Praise for

LOB

'An exquisite novel'
Sunday Telegraph

'Laced with poems, and beautifully illustrated, this is
a magical story of believing in the unknown'
Guardian

'Mystical and beautiful'
The Bookseller

'A family classic'
Observer

'Linda Newbery tells her story beautifully,
evoking empathy and emotion'
Scotsman

'There's something timeless about this lovely story'
The Ultimate Book Guide

www.**davidficklingbooks**.co.uk

Also by Linda Newbery:

The Shell House
Sisterland
Set in Stone
Flightsend

David Fickling Books
OXFORD · NEW YORK
31 Beaumont Street
Oxford OX1 2NP, UK

LOB
Linda Newbery

Illustrated by Pam Smy

LOB
A DAVID FICKLING BOOK 978 1 849 92049 0

Published in Great Britain by David Fickling Books,
a division of Random House Children's Books
A Random House Group Company

Hardback edition published 2010
This edition published 2011

5 7 9 10 8 6

Set in ITC New Baskerville

DAVID FICKLING BOOKS
31 Beaumont Street, Oxford, OX1 2NP

www.**kids**at**randomhouse**.co.uk
www.**randomhouse**.co.uk

Addresses for companies within The Random House Group Limited can be found at:
www.randomhouse.co.uk/offices.htm

THE RANDOM HOUSE GROUP Limited Reg. No. 954009

A CIP catalogue record for this book is available from the British Library.

The Random House Group Limited supports The Forest Stewardship
Council (FSC®), the leading international forest certification organisation.
Our books carrying the FSC label are printed on FSC® certified paper.
FSC is the only forest certification scheme endorsed by the leading
environmental organisations, including Greenpeace. Our
paper procurement policy can be found at
www.randomhouse.co.uk/environment

MIX
Paper from
responsible sources
FSC® C016897

Printed and bound in Great Britain by Clays Ltd, St Ives PLC

For the man who walks the roads

First light, first misted
light. Spill of dawn
along the valley fills
woods with birdsong.
The cottage sleeps.
Out here, the scritch
and creep and slither,
the skitter and croak
of being, bee-ing,
beetling, of spider,
of mouse, of frog.
Listen. Listen.

The song of the earth.

Part One

Early June

'Lob?' said Grandpa Will, in the summer garden. 'Oh, he's older than anyone can tell. Older than the trees. Older than anybody.'

'And what does he do?' asked Lucy. She knew the answer, but liked Grandpa to tell her.

'Lob-work, that's what he does. Odd jobs around the place.' He always said it like that – Lob-work. Whenever he and Lucy were out here, Grandpa would look at a well-tended onion bed, or a watering can filled and ready, and he'd smile. And sometimes he'd look towards the hedge, as if someone was there. When Lucy looked too, she'd see only a quiver in the leaves; a mouse,

13

perhaps, or a spider. The thing about Lob
was that not everyone could see him. Most
people couldn't.

'How long has Lob been here?' Lucy
asked. She knew the story, but liked hearing
it over and over again.

'Oh, a long, long time. Long before you
were born. Before your dad was born,'

Grandpa said, his voice settling comfortably into the telling. 'It was just after your gran and I got married, and came to live here. I was chopping wood one evening, when all of a sudden I knew I was being watched. So I stopped chopping and turned round. In the corner of my eye I saw him. There he stood' – he turned round to look – 'just there, by the bench. But I could only see him sidelong. When I stared straight at him, he faded away. Still, I knew who he was, knew at once. I'd heard about Lob from my grandfather, and he'd heard from *his* grandfather, and so on, back and back and back. There's always been Lob. He walks the roads, that's what he does. He walks and he walks, and he looks for the right person. When he finds that person, he stays around for a very long time. So I hoped he'd stay with me, and when he did I knew how lucky I was.'

'Lob chose you!'

'He did.'

'Will he always stay?'

'Till I die, I hope,' said Grandpa, looking round as if he wanted Lob to hear.

'But you're not going to die, are you, Grandpa?'

'We all will, in the end,' Grandpa said. 'But we needn't worry ourselves. I'm not expecting it for a while yet.'

They walked down to the end of the vegetable garden. Just the two of them, or perhaps it was the three of them.

'Is he here now?' Lucy asked, peering into the thicket of raspberry canes. 'Can you see him?'

'He'll be around somewhere. He don't always choose to be seen, Lob doesn't.'

'Will I see him?'

'I wouldn't be at all surprised,' said Grandpa. 'You're good at seeing.'

Lucy wanted and wanted and wanted to

be a Lob person. She squeezed her hands into fists with wanting; she clenched her eyes tight shut, and hoped that Lob would be there when she opened them.

He wasn't. But she was sure that one day he would be.

The others – Mum and Dad and Granny Annie – thought Lob was just a game, though Grandpa often mentioned him.

'It's lucky I've got Lob,' Grandpa would say, sitting down on the bench for a rest. 'I'd find it all a bit much, these days.' And always he said, 'Thank you, my friend' – first thing in the morning, and every time he finished work and went indoors.

'Don't fill the child's head with your nonsense!' Granny would tell him, tutting. And she'd look at Lucy and shake her head, smiling, as if Lucy was old enough to know better, and Grandpa was the child.

Whatever the grown-ups said, Lucy knew there was special magic here.

She knew it whenever she came to Granny and Grandpa's. On summer mornings, early, when the grass glittered with dew. On winter nights, looking through the window of her attic room. The darkness out there was giddy with stars, and she heard the cry of an owl, or a fox, or a something, from down in the woods.

Garden magic tingled through her, from her hair to her toe-nails.

Mum said that the magic was in Grandpa's fingers. Green fingers, Mum said he had. And Lucy giggled, imagining Grandpa with green pointy fingers like an elf. In fact his hands were square and stubby, with tough, cracked nails, from all the garden work he did. He had to do a lot of scrubbing to get his hands clean when he came indoors.

Every day, Grandpa Will worked on his vegetable patch. He grew peas and runner beans, raspberries and gooseberries, carrots and parsnips, lettuces and onions and

potatoes: all in neat rows, in beds that were perfectly dug and weeded.

It was a lot for him to do, all by himself. But of course, according to Grandpa, he didn't do it on his own; he was helped by Lob, in all sorts of ways. When Lob wasn't skittering about the woods or sleeping in the hedge, he found jobs to do. He collected logs, swept up piles of leaves, cleaned the tools, weeded the beds and picked off slugs and snails.

Lob only did it when no one was looking, Grandpa said. And only when he wanted.

'You can't give him orders, tell him what to do,' Grandpa told Lucy. 'He does what he likes, Lob does.'

Often, Lucy tried to spy on Lob, hoping for just a glimpse. She'd dart out of the back door, or stalk round the corner of the cottage. But she'd never seen him, no matter how hard she searched or how cold she got, lurking in wait.

It was the beginning of June. The sky stretched high and higher, streaked with cloud. Lucy and Grandpa Will were down in the garden, planting out runner beans. These leafy little plants had grown from the beans they'd sown in small pots, last time Lucy stayed. That was magic, if anything was!

20

The mottled pinkish beans
had been dry, rattling
from their packet as
Grandpa shook them
into his hand. Lucy
couldn't believe
there was life in
them, but Grandpa
soaked them over-
night, and next day
showed Lucy how
they'd plumped up,
how a tiny tip of root
was starting to feel its way. Now –
now look! There were leaves, and stems that
twined up their sticks, reaching for the sky.

Grandpa (and Lob, he said) had made the
soil ready, digging and digging, adding dark
compost, till the earth was as rich and moist
as fruit cake. He'd put up wigwams of canes
for the bean plants to climb. Now he and
Lucy worked together with trowel and

watering can. Lucy carried the plants to Grandpa, who tipped each one out of its pot, settled it in its hole, then pushed and firmed the soil with the tips of his fingers.

Lucy sprinkled water, making a small puddle round each plant.

'Will they grow?' she asked.

'Oh, they will, sure as ninepence,' said Grandpa.

Just then, Granny Annie shouted and waved at them from the back door. Someone had come from the village to see Grandpa.

'Want to carry on, Lucy love?' Grandpa straightened, and wiped his hands on his trousers. 'You know what to do.'

Lucy felt important. She had to do it right.

She crouched by the canes and reached for the trowel. When she'd dug the right-sized hole she filled it from her can; then, when the water had drained away, she copied Grandpa, tapping a plant free from its pot and holding it carefully in her hands.

She put it in the hole, and felt which way it wanted to face. Then she trowelled the earth around it, and pressed it close with her fingertips, as if tucking the plant up in bed.

'Grow!' she told it.

Had she done it well? Would the roots reach down, and the plant grow strong? Did she have magic in her fingers?

When she'd planted them all, she went to the water-butt by the shed to refill her can. It was heavy to carry, and she sloshed water into her shoes. Concentrating hard, she didn't notice at first, but then she did.

In the gooseberry bushes near the cane wigwams, there was a flicker of movement. A tremor of greeny-brown. The flash of an eye, a bright green eye. It looked at her and seemed amused by what it saw; then blinked, and was gone.

'Lob?' she whispered.

All she saw now was leaves and grass. The gooseberry stems prickled her hands as she

pushed them aside. Her ears caught a rustle that could have been laughter; then no more. Whatever it was, it was gone.

Lucy knew from Grandpa Will that Lob was a wild thing, who wouldn't let himself be caught or touched, or even stared at for long. But she'd seen him at last – seen him, all by herself! – and that made her feel special. Lob magic, garden magic – she was part of it now. It was part of her. She danced a little jig of celebration. When Grandpa came back to see how she was getting on, she rushed up to him.

'Grandpa, Grandpa! I've seen Lob!' She pulled at his sleeve, guiding him towards the gooseberries. 'There! He was sort of greeny, and he was looking at me. I think he was laughing.'

Grandpa was delighted. 'Yes! That's him, all right. Excellent! You're learning to see. I thought so. Most people don't. They look straight at Lob and have no idea he's there.'

Lucy soon realized that she wouldn't always see Lob; only sometimes, and only quick glimpses. Once she saw an old face, gnarled and barky; sometimes there was a shiver in the long grass, as if a snake was sliding through.

But even without seeing, Lucy knew he was there, from the way she felt inside. There was a sparking of mischief in her head, a tingle of energy in her arms and legs. She wanted to run, jump, climb, be everywhere at once. And she knew that Lob made Grandpa feel the same, even though he didn't run, or jump, or climb. He just moved around the grass paths and the tool shed in his usual way, slowly, surely and a little stiffly.

'Oh, you and your Lob!' the others would say to Grandpa – Dad, and Mum, and Granny Annie. They'd exchange grins that said *Let him play his little game.*

Lucy had to feel sorry for them. They

had no idea. And she and Grandpa Will exchanged secret smiles of their own.

In the car on the long journey back to London, Mum said, 'You know Lob's not real, don't you, Lucy-Lu? It's just Grandpa's story. He likes making up special stories, just for you. There isn't really a Lob.'

'But there is, there is! I've seen him!'

'No, Lucy, you haven't. Not really. You just think you have.'

Lucy began to fear they might be right. Was Lob just a game she played with Grandpa?

Next time she went to Clunny Cottage, she was afraid that the Lob feeling wouldn't be the same.

But – yes! As soon as she got out of the car, and stretched, and hugged Granny and Grandpa, she felt Lob-magic everywhere. In the quiver of a leaf. In the deep shadows of the ash tree. In the small breeze that stirred the leaves. Here he was. Her heart lifted; she felt it rise and swell in her chest, warming her with happiness. She felt bigger and more alive here than anywhere else.

'Hello, Lob,' she whispered.

Of course he was here. Of course he was real. Now, and for ever and ever and ever.

August

In the summer holidays, Lucy went to stay with Granny and Grandpa by herself. She loved that. She liked London and home, but she loved Clunny Cottage. Dawn crept early through her bedroom window, and the air outside was full of birdsong and baaing. Hedges ran greenly between fields dotted with sheep. When she looked out, she saw the trees all hazed with mist.

She heard the laughing yaffle of a wood-pecker, invisible in leafiness. Or was that Lob?

Later she went down into the garden with Grandpa to pick peas, choosing the plumpest pods. She liked to slit them with her thumb, and see the peas packed inside, like little green baubles.

The stream, close by, ran along the bottom of the garden. Sometimes it was a full brown swirl, sometimes just a shining thread. Lucy thought of all that water, how it knew which way to go. How it made its own pathways, deep and sure.

'Where does the water keep coming from?' she asked Grandpa. 'Won't it run out one day? What if it does?'

She heard a chittering laugh from the bushes that fringed the stream.

'Don't take any notice of Lob,' said Grandpa. 'He's being rude.'

'But will it?'

'No, Lucy-Lu. It never runs out. It comes from the rain on the hills. It trickles down the hillsides and into the stream, and the stream flows into the river, and into the sea. And the winds pick up water and make clouds and then it rains some more. And so it goes on.'

'For ever and ever and ever?'

'For ever and ever and ever,' said Grandpa. 'We'd better go in now, Lucy-Lu.

We need to get ourselves spruced up.'

They were going to a wedding that afternoon, in the village two miles away. After
lunch they all got dressed in their best
clothes. They stood in the kitchen looking
not quite like themselves: Granny Annie in a
flowery dress and a hat, and Grandpa
smarter than Lucy had ever seen him before,
in pressed trousers and a jacket and a
waistcoat and tie, and shoes polished to a
high shine. Lucy wore her blue dress, and a
hat with a rosebud pinned to its ribbon.

'Don't we look smart!' said Granny Annie,
and she giggled as she looked down at her
feet, in pink sandals.

'What are you laughing at?' Lucy asked.

'My feet,' Granny Annie explained. 'They
don't look like mine, all bunched up in posh
shoes.'

Lucy crouched to look. 'I think they *are*
yours, though.'

A horn beeped outside, and off they went

in someone's car.

Lucy thought the wedding was lovely, especially the bridesmaid's dress and posy. As she came out of the church, blinking in sunlight, Grandpa called her back. He wanted to show her something.

The stone arch of the door was all carved into leaves and acorns, berries and twining stems. Grinning down at Lucy, was a small carved face – a face masked by leaves, a face as old as the years and as young as Lucy.

She could easily have thought it winked at her. It reminded her of someone.

'Oh!' went Lucy, and then she whispered, 'Is it him?'

Grandpa nodded. 'See, someone knew him. Knew him well.'

'Someone a long, long time ago,' Lucy said.

'Yes, but someone as here as you and me.' Grandpa's fingers touched the smoothness of stone. '*Chip, chip, chip,* he went, and he made that face. Brought it out of the stone.'

'So is it Lob? Our Lob?'

'What have you found there?' said a man with hairy ears and a shiny purple tie, peering up. 'Ah! A Green Man. Rather a good one.'

No! It's Lob, Lucy thought. And the man was talking too loudly. Everyone would hear.

'But he isn't green.' She spoke very quietly, so that the man had to bend his head to listen. 'He's stone.'

'Yes, but he's still a Green Man,' said the man, who obviously thought he knew what was what, and didn't expect anyone to argue. 'See the leaves? One does come across them occasionally.'

Grandpa only nodded and smiled. Lucy frowned.

'D'you mean you've seen one in real life?' she asked sharply. Surely this loud, confident man wasn't a Lob kind of person.

'Of course not!' The man looked down his nose at her; it was the kind of nose that made her think what a peculiar thing a nose was. 'They're only make-believe. No more real than fairies and leprechauns. You see them carved in wood or stone.'

He glanced at Grandpa, who only smiled, and gave Lucy a look that said *we know better*.

Lucy felt sorry for this man who could see carvings in wood or stone but not the real thing, so she gave him a pitying look as everyone lined up for the photographer in front of the church. She was pleased about the *make-believe*. People might talk knowledgeably about Green Men, might see stone faces – but the real, living Lob was her secret. Hers and Grandpa Will's.

The photographer waved his hand to make them all huddle up tight. 'Ready, everyone? Don't say cheese, say *sausages*.'

There they all are, in the wedding photo in Granny Annie's album. Everyone's doing *sausages* grins at the camera. Lucy's smiling, too, but she's glancing off to one side. Looking back at that Green Man, to see if he's trying to catch her eye.

Late October

At autumn half-term, Lucy and Dad stayed three nights at Clunny Cottage.

The days were golden, long-shadowed. Down in the orchard, the boughs of the apple trees were heavy with fruit. The branches were so low that, without even stretching, Lucy could hold an apple in her hand and give a little twist to make it drop. Wasps buzzed and drowsed, making fruity caves in fallen apples and plums.

Granny Annie made apple pie, and plum crumble, and blackberry jam. Dusk came early, and the cottage seemed to shrug into itself. Grandpa chopped wood and lit a log fire.

They'd picked and eaten the last of the
runner beans that Lucy had sown and
planted; now she and Grandpa collected
potatoes. Grandpa thrust his fork into the
ground, wriggled it and lifted. Potatoes
tumbled free, smooth as eggs, clodded with
soil. Lucy gathered them, brushed off the
earth, and dropped them into a bucket.
Grandpa dug up carrots too, but he said the
parsnips would be best left a bit longer.

'What does Lob do in winter?' Lucy took off her muddy shoes, and stowed them under the bench.

'Oh, he don't do much when winter comes,' said Grandpa Will. 'Not once all the leaves are swept, and the logs in, and we're tucked up snug. He likes to lie by the fire, night-times. He'll stir himself to do a few jobs on warmer days, but mainly he sleeps. Rests. Gets his energy back. He'll have earned it. He's worked hard this year.'

Sometimes Lucy saw Lob as a bent old man; sometimes as a flitty green thing like a dragonfly, quick and agile, young as herself, or younger.

'Will he be around for ever and ever?'

Grandpa nodded. 'I hope so. He never gets older, see. Every year he comes back, full of spring. Full of growing.'

After tea, the dusk drew Lucy outside. She sneaked out of the cottage when no one was looking. Down the garden she went, along the mown path.

There was a rustle by the compost heap, a ripple through the long grass. Lob was there. Lucy couldn't see him, but she knew he was pleased and boastful, full of pride in the glory of the garden and its harvest, his work well done. He darted and scurried and skittered ahead and alongside, he chivvied her from behind. Lucy laughed, and pretended to be frightened.

She crossed the stream, treading carefully on the stepping stones. It would be too cold to fall in now.

Knowing she shouldn't, she took the leafy path into the woods, and stood in the thick of the trees. No one knows where I am, she thought: only Lob. And there was a deliciousness about that, salted with fear. She could run back, if she wanted. In the kitchen the light was on behind drawn curtains; Dad was washing up, and Granny

Annie putting things away. Or had they finished now? Would they come looking for her?

The gap between indoors and out, tameness and wildness, lightness and dark, stretched wide and wider in the flittery dusk. Lucy didn't want to go in, not yet. Stars were pricking the sky, tree branches stretching out to muffle them.

It was colder than she'd realized. A thorn snagged her sleeve. As she tried to free herself, her foot sank into soft mud. She jumped back as a stinging nettle seared her wrist. Perhaps she didn't like it here after all, not on her own. Where was he? Where was Lob?

A face was looking down at her, a face in the trees – a gnarled, knobbled, grizzled face. It scowled and grimaced, but no, that couldn't be Lob. Lob was farther on, laughing at her for being scared. He dared her to go on.

41

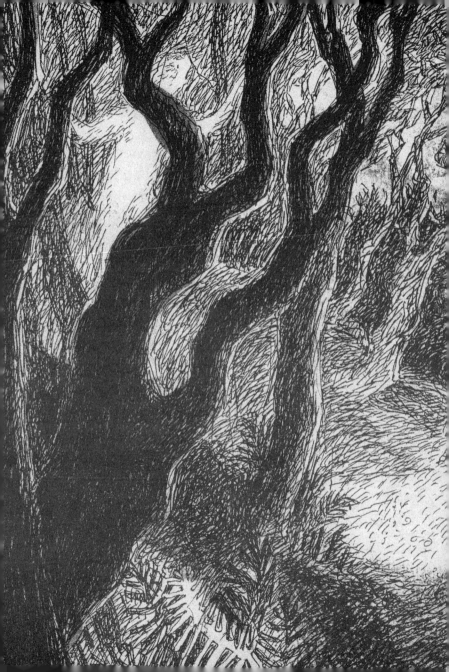

But I won't, Lucy decided. He'd get her into trouble. It was all right for Lob; he didn't have to think about getting told off, or being lost in the dark. She pulled her foot out of the mud with a *plotch*, and began feeling her way back to the stepping stones. Which way? This way? Or was that farther into the wood?

'Lucy?' came Grandpa's voice, through the trees.

'Lucy-Lu?' called Dad's. And she saw the bobbing light of a torch beam.

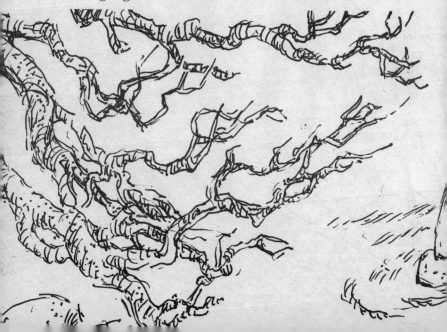

'I'm here!' she shouted back, trying to sound brave.

And by the time they reached her, she'd crossed the stream and was back in the orchard, pretending not to have been far.

Dad was cross with her for going out in the dark on her own. She didn't make excuses, didn't try to blame it on Lob or on anyone but herself.

'You're all right,' Grandpa said, but she heard the shakiness in his voice, as if he was the one who'd been frightened. Indoors, he

made hot chocolate for everyone.

Lucy was glad to be back by the warmth of the fire, but she hugged to herself the thrill of being out in the dark, with Lob and the trees and the stars. Her wrist burned with the sting of the nettle.

'What's Lob made of?' she asked Grandpa, on the last morning, while they were eating breakfast.

'Ah, well now.' Grandpa sliced the top off his boiled egg, then paused. 'It's hard to say. But I'll try.'

Granny Annie, on her way to refill the kettle, tutted and looked at Dad, who shook his head in a weary *must we?* way. Lucy waited. Grandpa leaned towards her, as if to share a secret.

'See, he's made of rain and wind,' he told her. 'And sun, and hail. And light and dark. There's fire in him too, and earth and air. He's made of grit and stones, and stardust.

And time gone and time waiting. Come to think of it, that's the same as all of us.' He looked surprised to have said so much, then added: 'That's all I know.' And he reached for the pepper pot.

'Very nice, Dad,' said Lucy's dad. 'If Lob existed, I'm sure that's how he'd be.'

'How he *is*,' said Lucy, and she looked across the table at Grandpa. He grinned back, then sprinkled pepper on his egg, and dipped a finger of toast.

Soon, too soon, the getting into the car, the waving goodbye. The *Look after yourselves* and the *Bye-bye, lovey* and the *See you at Christmas*. Lucy didn't know whether she was happier or sadder. She was going home, and that was where she belonged, with Mum and Dad. But she was leaving Clunny Cottage, and she belonged here too. Couldn't she split herself in half, and be in both places at once?

As the car pulled away, she looked out of the window for the very last glimpse of Clunny Cottage, and Granny and Grandpa at the gate, and maybe Lob as well. They waved, and she waved back until the car turned a bend in the lane and she couldn't see them any more.

Dad knew it made Lucy sad to leave, so he said, as he always did, 'We'll be back soon as soon, Lucy-Lu.'

End of November

Then, four weeks later, the news: the awful, unbelievable news. The news that meant nothing would ever, ever, ever be the same again.

A phone call, from tearful Granny. Grandpa Will had been pulling leeks in the morning, and by afternoon he was dead.

A heart attack.

Lucy's mind froze in bewilderment.

Grandpa had died.

Gone.

Gone.

Gone where?

She'd never see him again, never hear his voice.

Never.

Grandpa Will. Her Grandpa.

They couldn't move away from the phone. Dad sat on the stairs and cuddled Lucy and

Mum both together. Lucy was too numb to cry until she saw Mum and even Dad crying. Then they all cried together, sharing a box of tissues.

'It's the way he'd have wanted,' Dad said, in a voice that wavered. 'Dropping dead with his boots on, pulling up a good crop of leeks. He'd have hated to get old and ill and have to go into a home or a hospital. He'd have hated not being able to grow his veg, or hear his birds.'

Next day they went back to Clunny Cottage to help Granny Annie with everything that had to be done.

The cottage felt so different without Grandpa Will. Sad. Silent. Empty, even with Granny and Mum and Dad and Lucy there. There was something different in the way they spoke to each other. A strange echo. An emptiness that should have been filled with Grandpa.

And Lob? Where was he?

Lucy stood outside in the vegetable garden. The soil was dug and weeded, the sprouts and onions in neat rows, the watering cans full and ready. Lob-work, surely.

'Lob!' Lucy called, in a whisper, not wanting the grown-ups to hear.

He must be as sad as she was. As lost. What would he do without Grandpa?

'Lob!' she called again. 'Are you there?'

Did she see a shiver in the beech hedge, a quiver of dry leaves?

She waited, but Lob didn't appear. It was too cold to stand outside for long.

Indoors, the grown-ups talked and talked. People came to visit, speaking in hushed, solemn voices. The postman brought cards.

There was a funeral in the village church-yard. Grandpa, in his coffin, was lowered into the ground.

No, no, you can't do that! That's my Grandpa! Lucy wanted to shout. It was all a terrible mistake.

She stood holding Granny's hand, while tears ran down her face and splashed off her chin. It was a golden winter's day, long-shad-owed, a day Grandpa would have loved. An afternoon for sitting on his bench with a mug of tea, looking with satisfaction at the work he'd done. Rooks cawed high in the trees.

Why wasn't Grandpa here? Where was he?

Lucy caught sight of a gnarled face peeping from the shadows of the yew tree.

She'd thought Lob was always at Clunny Cottage, in the garden or down in the

woods. But, yes, the churchyard was a
Lob-place, full of growing: the twisted yew
tree that was hundreds
of years old, the
tall nettles by
the compost
heap, the holly
bright with
berries.

Carved in the
church porch was
the stone man
that someone
had made
hundreds of
years ago.
Chip, chip, chip,
he went, Grandpa
had said,
someone as here
as you and me. And the face in the stone
would last for ever and ever.

January

Everything was changing, all the things
Lucy had thought would always be the
same. Granny Annie decided that she didn't
want to stay at Clunny Cottage by herself.

'I'd be lonely without Will, all by myself.
And the garden's too big to manage.'

Instead, she moved to a smaller cottage in
the village, with friendly neighbours on each
side, and a shop across the street. Early in
the new year, Mum and Dad and Lucy
helped her to pack up and move.

Lucy hated seeing Clunny Cottage bare
and empty. All her Grandpa Will thoughts
had nowhere to be.

'*We* could come and live here!' she told
her parents. 'Couldn't we? It'd be nice and
close to Granny.'

Mum gave her a cuddle. 'Sweetheart, you
know we can't. Yes, it'd be lovely, but Dad

and I have to be in London. We couldn't get jobs here, miles from anywhere.'

But what about Lob?

Lucy needed to know, but there was no one to ask – no one who understood. There's only Grandpa, she thought. So Grandpa was the person she asked, silently, standing outside the back door.

The weather had turned so cold and wintry that summer seemed impossible. The dug beds were frozen into hard clumps. Every leaf, every blade of grass, had a rim of frost, like icing sugar.

Grandpa Will, Lucy said, in her thoughts, *what will Lob do when spring comes and you're not here?*

He'll walk, said Grandpa's voice in her head. *He'll walk the roads. He'll look for his special person. When he finds that person, he'll stay.*

It was a comfort, the way she could bring Grandpa back. Hear his voice so clearly, and the things he'd said. But she hated to think of Lob finding someone else.

But I *want to be Lob's special person! I don't* want *him to find someone new!*

And this time Grandpa didn't answer.

'Lob,' she whispered, and her breath plumed up in a cloud. 'Are you there? Are you listening? Come to London. I'll be your person.'

But what if Lob was hibernating? Not there to listen? When he woke up, he might think she'd gone away without even saying goodbye.

In her rucksack she had a little notebook with a pen attached. She sat on the bench to write a letter. Her fingers were almost too cold to grip the pen, but she wrote as neatly as she could.

Dear Lob,

You must be lonley without Grandpa. I miss him too. Why don't you come and live in London? That's where I live. It's not as green as you're used to and we haven't got a garden. But there's a park near our house with a lake. There's trees and grass and bushes too. It's called Leaside Park and it's near the station. I'll look out for you there.

Here she stopped and thought. Lob could come with them in the car, but she was quite sure he wouldn't – Grandpa said he'd walk the roads. Besides, he had a habit of flicking and darting away when you tried to look at him properly – you couldn't get nearer than he wanted. He'd never let himself be trapped in the back seat of a car.

She wrote:

It's a long walk though and I don't realy know the way. You need to get on the Moter Way and then you'll see signs that point to London.

Please come. I could be your special person. Can I?

It's been good playing with you. Thanks for helping Grandpa. Take care,

Lucy xxx

She whisper-read it aloud, just in case Lob was listening.

Then, carefully, she pulled the page loose from the notebook, folded it up very small, and tucked it under one foot of the bench, where no one but Lob would find it.

Grandpa's ash tree was bare, but already its coal-black buds were about to burst into leaf. The yearly miracle, Grandpa called it.

'Lucy! Are you out there? We're ready to go,' Dad called from indoors.

'Goodbye, Lob,' Lucy whispered. 'I'll be looking for you.'

Part Two

Early February

100

Winter. Hard-frozen, deep-shrunken resting time. Twigs bare, earth clodded, grass bleached pale. Early dark, early to roost. Moon sails high, star-map glitters cold over the hills. Fox-shape slinks through the dark.

Change is coming. The smell of change spikes the air.

Lob was older than anyone could know. Not as old as the hills, but much older than the trees. Not as old as life, but much older than anyone living. Not as old as death, but far, far older than anyone born.

Although he'd lived in a lot of different places, he didn't change willingly. He might well have stayed longer at Clunny Cottage before setting off to find a new person. But something happened to make that impossible.

When Granny Annie moved to her new home in Clunton, the landlord sold the cottage and its garden to a builder, making himself a lot of money. A SOLD notice went up, and a sign saying that four brand-new

houses were to be built.

It was a grey, bleak February, and Lob
spent much of the time sleeping in the
cottage eaves. With no fire to lie by, he'd
gone shrunken and small, weakened by
winter and cold weather.

Usually, at this time of year, on the days
when it wasn't quite so cold, he'd look after
the cabbages and the purple-sprouting
broccoli. He'd turn over the leaf mould, and
make sure Will's tools and pots were clean
and ready. But now there were no tools.
They'd been taken away when the cottage
was emptied.

Lob waited.

After a while, a digger arrived, and
moved with dinosaur slowness into Will's
vegetable beds. Into *Lob's* vegetable beds.
Lob watched, outraged.

Roaring yellow
monster, slow moving,
quick turning. Treads
crush life. Head rears
high, giant teeth gape.
Fangs gouge,
wrench,
tear. Stems
and roots
and leaves
mashed and
mangled
in monster
jaws.

Run at it, shout, batter with fists. Monster trundles on. Clumsy blind brute.

The digger driver wasn't the sort of person who could see Lob. His radio was on in the cab, and he whistled cheerfully while he worked. He had no idea of the fierce little figure that rushed at him, green eyes glittering.

At last the digger trundled off down the road, scattering strips of pressed mud.

Lob stood looking at the devastation. If he'd been given to despair, he would have despaired now. Instead he began tidying as best he could, collecting bits of twig and root, heaping them ready to be burned.

But it wasn't finished yet. Two days later, more strangers came to Clunny Cottage.

Some were smartly dressed, and carried boards with papers clipped to them; others wore helmets and bright yellow jackets. They went inside the cottage, making loud remarks that echoed emptily.

Then they surrounded the ash tree, and one of the men chalked a red cross on its bark. The ash tree that had stood for more than a hundred years, shading Clunny Cottage, was in the way of the new houses, so it had to go.

Next day the executioners arrived, three of them. One slapped his hand against the mark on the tree's trunk, then rubbed the chalk off his palm. Another carried a heavy saw with crocodile teeth. Lob flung himself at them, waved his arms, shouted and stamped, but no one noticed.

The saw whined and screamed. Sharp teeth bit into bark. The shock juddered deep into the ground.

The tree tried to stand tall, but was wounded too badly. Soon it surrendered. Groans shuddered through every twig. Its leaves twitched and writhed, its branches sagged. The core of its trunk screeched in agony.

At last the butchers had finished their work. They drank coffee from their flasks; they laughed and joked together.

When they'd gone, leaving the wreckage of branches and twigs strewn over the ground, Lob crept away.

Now? Where?

He stood by the gate and heard the call of the road. He hadn't walked for many years, but roads were deep inside him. His feet knew their tread and their hardness, their forks and their bends, their uphills and downs, and their long reach into places he didn't know yet.

The soles of his feet were starting to prickle. Time to go.

Lob walked away from Clunny Cottage without looking back.

February

At home in London, Lucy wasn't well. She felt dizzy. She had a high temperature. Her throat was sore, and her head ached.

'Better stay home today,' Mum said, shaking the thermometer.

Lucy wasn't often ill, and didn't like to miss school. But she felt peculiar. When she stood up, her head went floaty and her legs seemed to have no bones in them. She clambered back into bed.

She dozed and she dreamed. Sometimes she lay awake.

'Would you like a book to read?' Dad asked when she woke up. 'Shall I read a story?'

Lucy shook her head. What she wanted was Grandpa to tell her a Lob story. And those were stored in her memory.

Oh yes, there's always been Lob. He's hundreds

and hundreds of years old, said Grandpa's voice in her head. *Old as the hills.*

No, Lob won't die, said Grandpa. *He'll go on and on living, as long as the Earth is green.*

Green-fingered, that's Lob, said Grandpa. *You know how people say that? Lob's got greener fingers than anyone. What he does is, he collects seeds and keeps them in his pockets. Then he scatters them as he walks. That's why you sometimes see wild flowers sprouting out of pavements and walls. Lob-work.*

Yes. Yes. Lucy listened to the stories in her head. She smiled and she dreamed and she gazed at nothing till her eyes went funny.

'It's shock, I'm sure,' Mum said. 'The shock of losing Grandpa.'

When Lucy felt a bit better and could sit up in bed, she asked for her coloured pencils, and paper for drawing. She tried to draw Lob, but that was difficult, as she'd had only glimpses. She drew a jumble

of green and brown
leaves, and bright
eyes peering.

LOB, she
wrote under-
neath.

'Yes, it's a nice way
of remembering Grandpa,'
said Dad, looking.
'He was good, wasn't he,
with his stories? Almost made us all
believe in Lob.'

'Lob's real,' Lucy said fiercely.

'Don't you know that? You ought to.'

Dad looked at her, and she saw his mouth move to say something, but then he only smiled.

She knew he wouldn't argue while she was ill.

As soon as she could get out of bed without feeling giddy, she went to the window and pushed back the curtains. It was dusk. In the light of the street lamp, she saw the shiver of bare twigs. Spring would come soon. Lob time. Time for Lob to be busy. Even here on the London street, things were growing.

When would he be here? How long would it take?

'Please come, Lob,' she whispered. 'I'll wait for you.'

February

The road's calling.
A wash of light in the
east, and a taste of
spring in the air. Road
dips and rises, dives
through trees, curves
over a hill. Back and
forth in time it leads.
The current of feet and
wheels have worn it
smooth.

  Boot soles tingle to the

call of the road.
There's only one way
to go.
Walk. Walk the road.

Lob walked with a steady, plodding gait. He never hurried. He never dawdled. He never stopped to get his breath back, even on the steepest hill. He walked and he walked.

He didn't know where he was going, but he'd know when he got there.

There were cars everywhere nowadays. They came, passed by, and were gone, leaving the tang of fuel and the thrum of engines. With each passing, it took minutes for the quiet to ebb back. Then the air was disturbed only by birdsong and baaing and the steady, steady tread of Lob's boots walking.

In the cars there were faces. Often a pair of

eyes swept over and through Lob, unseeing.

When he'd put several miles behind him,
Lob reached a small town. Here the road
from the valley joined another, a bigger one.

South. South. He could go in any direction
he chose, but something was calling him to
the south.

He tramped on, alongside the swish and
hum of passing traffic. He kept a wary
margin between the road and himself. He'd
seen a dead and bloodied badger, and a
flattened squirrel, and knew that those
speeders could crush and kill.

A sharp east wind was gusting; winter
wasn't yet gone. But the first buds were in
the hedgerows like green candle flames.
The hedge sparrows and wrens were busy,
and the starlings and the rooks, the
robins and the finches. They knew it would
be spring soon.

From time to time Lob dipped into his
pocket for seeds to sprinkle by the roadside.

Willowherb and grass, sweet rocket and ox-eye daisy seed he scattered like pepper dust. He plucked a young cabbage from a field, and crunched it right down to the core as he walked; he drank from a stream.

As dusk fell he looked for somewhere to sleep, and came to a green mound, an island in the road. Rabbits had nibbled the grass close and left neat pellets. Trees and shrubs had been planted in a ring. In the middle was a grassy hollow, inviting to a weary wanderer.

He slept soundly. Next morning he walked on.

What was he looking for? He'd know when he found it. And towards next evening, he came to a place that promised shelter and maybe more.

Stony track to a lit shed. Glow of busyness. Lamplight and shadows. Dusty air loud with the *brurr* of ewes and the *meh!* of lambs. Man in shirtsleeves, hefting hay. Dog lying still. Watchful eyes see this stranger, not-stranger. Hackles rise, then tail thumps a welcome.

Woolly new life, eager to begin. First steps on trembly legs. Warmth and birth, blood and milk, straw and dung. Work to be done.

March

As soon as Lucy felt better, she made Dad take her to the park.

Dad had been a country boy, growing up at Clunny Cottage, so he liked parks and green places. He knew the names of the trees and the bushes, and all the different kinds of ducks and geese that came to the lake. He and Lucy took bread crusts to throw to the birds.

Spring was in the air. They heard it in the quacking of ducks and the cheeping of sparrows. They felt it in the breeze that came over the lake.

But where's Lob?

Lucy looked for him in the shrubs, and in the thicket of trees that ran along the railings. She listened for the scuffle of his tread and the rustle of his laugh.

She saw a magpie, she saw a squirrel, she

saw a blackbird, but she didn't see Lob. She
went home disappointed. Spring was Lob
time. Where was he? When would he come?

It was no use asking Dad. He knew lots of
things, but he didn't know Lob.

Next week at school, when it was the turn of
Lucy's class to make the mural for the hall,
the Green Man she'd seen at the church was
in her mind. Perhaps he'd been there all
the time.

The theme was spring, and a whole wall was to be taken up with a painting and collage. Some people painted enormous trees; others made leaves or daffodils. One group painted a lake, and pasted on lilies, ducks and fish.

Lucy worked on her own. She mixed paint in shades of rich green, and covered sheets of paper. When the paint was dry, she cut out lots of leaves. She arranged them around a face, a face with bright eyes and a grinning mouth. This face was so small and so green that

you wouldn't notice it unless
you looked into the leaves
very closely.

'Lucy's leaves can go here,
next to the gate,' called
the teacher, when it was
time to put the mural
together. She hadn't
noticed the face. No
one did; it was so
well hidden.

But every time
Lucy sat in assembly, she could look
across at her own Green Man, her own Lob.
Sometimes, she almost thought one of the
eyes winked at her.

She'd have to make do with this, till Lob
turned up in person.

May

Lob stayed at the sheep farm until all the lambs were born and out in the fields.

The year had rolled on. The sky was big and dark, here in the open country, and he'd seen the winter stars – hunter, dogs, swan – wheel round in their huge, slow arc.

Lob had been busy, all through lambing time. There were warm places to sleep, and turnips and swedes to eat. But he hadn't found his person. The sheep farmer, a nice enough man, never knew Lob was there.

They spent hours together, day and night, and Lob made himself useful in all sorts of ways – fetching water, guiding a bleary lamb to its mother, cleaning the pens, carrying straw. But the farmer wasn't a noticing sort of chap, and he never guessed how much he was being helped. He wasn't the Person for Lob.

Early one morning Lob walked up the track to the busy road he'd left, weeks ago. He stood and sniffed.

May time now, the best of May, the coolest, mistiest, grassiest time of summer. Hedge

snowed with hawthorn,
air silvered with
warbler-song. Daisies
wait for the sun. Hot
days and harvest to
come.

Work here's done.
The road's calling.

South. South. Head
south, to the glittering
city, the snaking river,
where roads run
together like the
centre of a web.

The road leads south,
the rushing trains, the
humming and buzzing
in the wires.
Walk. Walk.

Lob walked and he walked, with his steady
gait, never hurrying, never dawdling. He was
strong now, full of spring.

After many miles, curiosity drew him to a
field of concrete, where a large number of
cars and lorries had turned off the road.

Hundreds of them! The cars were packed
almost solid, while lorries and trucks had
gathered at one end. People made their way
to and from a long, low building, connected
by a bridge to another, exactly the same, on
the other side of the road.

It was the smell of hot food that pulled

Lob inside. He was hungry now, and tired.

No one in the motorway services saw the strange figure moving through the tables, the flit and dart of him. No one saw the flash of Lob's startling green eyes. No one pointed at him as he tasted leftover food on plates and trays – bits of blueberry muffin, salad, pizza crusts. No one wondered where he came from, or where he was going.

Once he'd eaten, and filled his pockets with bits of pizza crust, Lob began looking for the way out. He had no wish to stay in this strange place.

Too many, too crowded, too loud, too hot, too bright. No place for a traveller.

Escape, out into air.
Breathe.

Dazzle of sun on steel,
sun on glass. Heat
strikes baked concrete.
Squish of wheels, snarl
of engines.

Nowhere to hide.

May

Lucy woke up from a very sad dream. Her cheeks were wet and her eyes ached.

In her dream, she was back at Clunny Cottage, looking for Grandpa. She looked upstairs and down; she went outside, searched the garden and down in the woods, calling and calling. Round every corner she expected to see him; but he was nowhere.

'You won't find him here,' said a grown-up voice. 'Grandpa's died – didn't you know? He's not coming back.'

But that didn't make sense! He had to be *somewhere*.

Lucy hauled herself into wakefulness. She blinked, sat up and rubbed her eyes, thinking *What a horrible dream! But I'm awake now, and Grandpa's—*

And the shock of knowing whumped into her all over again.

She hadn't really meant to, but later that day she found herself telling her friend Trudie about Lob.

At least, she'd thought Trudie was her friend.

'What's that you're drawing?' Trudie asked, leaning across to look at Lucy's jotter. They always shared the same table.

'Oh! Nothing.' Lucy leaned forward, cradling her elbow.

'It's not nothing. Let's see.' Trudie edged closer, tugging the book from under Lucy's arm. 'Who's it meant to be?'

Lucy looked round to check that no one was listening. 'It's – someone very special. Someone only I know about, and Grandpa Will. It's our secret.'

'But your Grandad's dead!' said Trudie, in her blunt way.

'I know! But we've still got our secret, him and me. It's—' Lucy didn't want to say Lob's name out loud. 'It's this – well, sort of person. He's always around, but only Grandpa and I can see him. He was Grandpa's helper. He did all sorts of jobs. He makes things grow. He's been around for ever and ever. But only special people can see him.'

'And he looks like this?' Trudie squinted at Lucy's sketch. 'What is he, a little green

man? Shouldn't he have pointy ears, like an elf?'

'No! He's not like that.'

Lucy wished she hadn't said anything at all. She was glad when the bell went for playtime.

But all through play, and all through lunchtime, there was whispering and giggling. Trudie told Anisha, and Anisha told Karl, and Karl told Tomas, and soon everyone was teasing and taunting Lucy. 'Lucy believes in fairies! Lucy thinks she's got *fairies* in her garden! Little green men!'

Lucy felt the hurt of betrayal like a thump in her chest. She picked up her books and her pencil case and went to sit at a different table. For the rest of the day she refused to speak to Trudie – except to hiss at her, while they were changing for PE: 'You told my secret! I thought you were my friend!'

100

'You didn't say I couldn't!' huffed Trudie. 'Anyway, I bet you were only making it up.'

Lucy was silent for a moment. Then she said, 'Fooled you, though, didn't I? *Hahahahaha!*' she went, in the horrid cackly way she hated when other people did it. 'Who's silly now?'

By the time they went home, they were almost friends again. But now Lob was the one Lucy was cross with.

What was keeping him? Why hadn't he come? How long would it take him to walk all those miles? She had no idea, but surely he'd be here, if he was coming.

What if – she didn't want to let the thought into her head, but it was there now.

Wasn't it – perhaps – a bit childish to believe that Lob was real, that he was coming to find her?

What if Lob was just a game she used to play with Grandpa?

May

Dave and Mike were on their way to the
Chelsea Flower Show, with a truck packed
full of plants. They'd stopped at the services
for a break, but now Dave was overcome
with tiredness; he was fast asleep in the
driver's seat, one arm dangling from the
open window. Mike went round to the back
and let the ramp down, wanting to check
that none of the trees or shrubs had fallen
over. Everything seemed OK.

He sat on the ramp to finish his cold
drink. Being a gardener, he could
easily have been the sort of person
who'd see Lob, but he noticed
nothing. To him and Dave,
a travelling garden was nothing
out of the ordinary.

To Lob, it was a wonderful
piece of luck.

A shadowy cave!
Green, green, green.
    Cool and damp.
    Silver birch,
    hornbeam.
    Freckly foxgloves.
    Brush of leaves,
    moonshine of
    birch bark. Root
balls pillowed
in sacking.
    Leaf mould
breathes a welcome.

Leaves stir. Hush, hush. A place to rest. A haven, a couch, a bed.

Step inside. Settle, sigh. Sleep.

Mike didn't see the greenish person sidling up the ramp; didn't hear the sounds of comfortable settling against a root ball. Upending his bottle, he didn't hear Lob's light snoring.

So of course, when he got up to go, slammed the ramp and fastened it, Mike didn't know he was shutting anyone in.

CREAK – SCREECH – BLUNK!

Whhhh—? went Dave in the front, and Lob in the back, both of them jolted awake and boggle-eyed.

'Come on, mate. I'll drive if you want,' Mike told Dave. 'We'd best get moving.'

Blearily, Dave moved over; Mike climbed into the driver's seat and started up.

For hours, the lorry rumbled south. Shut in the back, Lob was dismayed at first, then baffled, then curious. What was this rolling forest? But the leaves of the trees and shrubs made a pleasant light tussling that made his surroundings seem almost normal. His instincts told him he was heading south, and that was the way he wanted to go.

They reached a city; Lob could sense it: the buildings crowding in, and the concretey smell. The lorry slowed, and crawled with other traffic.

When at last they came to a standstill, and the lorry gave a final shudder and was quiet, it was night-time. Hearing voices at the front,

Lob listened keenly.

'Not unloading now, are we?' said Dave's voice.

'Nah! It'll have to wait,' answered Mike's. 'Let's go and get some kip.'

And, murmuring together, the voices moved farther off.

Night went by, the short early-summer night. Lob ate the crusts and crumbs from his pockets, and waited. He could smell grass, and trees, and river, with only a faint city tang.

At last, at long last, there was a squeal and grind at the back of the lorry as the ramp was unbolted. Then the thump as it was lowered to the ground. Lob blinked in the dazzle of a bright morning. Stiffly he stretched himself and stood, then edged down the ramp, brushing between Dave

and Mike who were coming up.
Anyone would have thought
it   a strange sight, where Lob found
himself now. In this London park close to
the river, a huge white marquee was being
erected. All around it, stands were being put
up, lorries unloaded, and gardens made.

People scurried about like ants when their
nest is disturbed. They carried things to and
fro, called to each other, had busy conversa-
tions and arguments. They carted sacks and
tools and fence-posts. They stretched hoses
and buried electrical cables. Cranes
lowered full-grown trees into new
positions. Lob couldn't work
out what was going on.
Farming? Gardening?

But he knew farming, and he knew gardening, and this wasn't much like either. A new, city kind of farming? But farming was slow, and gardening was slow, and slow was the only way it could be. There was a lot of waiting, a lot of sprouting and growing and seeding, all at the proper time. *This* was all happening at high speed. The worker-ant people scurried about, all day long. Planks were hammered, paths laid, pagodas built. Statues and sculptures were heaved into place. The park was being turned into a garden of gardens, each one separate, each one different.

Dave and Mike were busy with a project of their own, a roped-off plot to transform into a woodland garden. It all had to be done in just a few days, ready for the show to open. They carried the trees into position, and consulted their plan.

'Here? Or here?'

'No, left a bit, so the branches hang over the path.'

They worked hard, carrying dozens of pots and sacks of compost. Carefully they tucked each plant into place. They covered root balls and pots with soil, so that the plants seemed to be growing in the ground.

Things were shaping up better than they'd expected. From time to time, Dave had the odd feeling that jobs were being done before he'd even thought of them: stray pots tidied, soil patted smooth, even the kettle filled ready to be boiled on the camping stove. Next morning, he found all their tools cleaned and polished and hung in their places in the van.

'Have you been working all night, or what?' Dave asked Mike, blinking, astonished.

'Not me, mate! Unless we did all this in our sleep?'

And their woodland garden looked, almost magically, like real woodland, like a forest you could wander into and get lost. The winding path had only been made yesterday,

but it looked like years and years
of leaf-fall. The trees cast dappled
shade; a butterfly settled on silver
bark. All the leaves were rain-fresh,
though neither Mike nor Dave had
heard rain in the night.

'What a team, eh?' Mike clapped Dave
on the back. 'We've done a great job.'

'It's like it made itself,' said Dave. And
they strolled off to the catering tent for a
celebratory beer.

Lob set off, exploring.

As he entered the big marquee, someone
was watching him. Watching with keenly
sharpened interest.

Late May

Lucy was walking home through the park, as she often did, with Trudie, Trudie's mum, and Trudie's brother Max in his buggy.

The park was an oasis of green in the city – that's what Grandpa had said, when he came to visit. There were mossy tree trunks, and branches that spread high. There was a corner where the grass grew long, full of buttercups and cow parsley. A squirrel ran across the grass, stopped,  and bushed its tail into a question mark. The park was full of growing, full of lushness and leafiness.

This was a Lob-place if ever there was one.

'Lob?' Lucy whispered, for no one to hear.

Instead of going over to the swings with

the others, she went to the edge of the trees. She dumped her bag. She picked up stones and dried leaves, bits of twig. Her fingers began shaping them into a pattern – a face, a Lob face. Maybe she could make a spell, a charm, to bring him here?

'Lob?' she whispered. 'Please?'

She shaped eyes and a nose. A mouth.

But she'd looked for Lob so many times, and he was never here. She ought to know by now. He wasn't coming, was he? He wasn't coming.

What was the point of pretending? Playing games with herself?

'Lucy? Come and have a drink,' called Trudie's mum, unpacking flasks and biscuits. Max squealed on the swing, clasped tightly by Trudie, who had him on her lap.

'What you doing, Lucy?' shouted Trudie.

'Oh, nothing!'

Trudie knew Lucy's *nothings*. She lifted Max down from the swing and went over to see.

Lucy stood up from crouching, and looked at the stones and sticks on the grass, because suddenly that's all they were. No spell, no magic. Not even really a face. Just a muddly mess of sticks and stones.

She felt herself burning with hurt. She jumped hard into the middle of the face; she kicked and she stamped. She was angry with Lob, with herself, with Trudie – even with Grandpa, for dying. For leaving her.

'Lucy dancing!' shouted Max, and he ran to join in.

Lucy trampled and trod. She kicked and scraped until nothing but broken sticks and pebbles showed where the face had been.

Late May

Indoor forest. Scents and fruits, glossy leaves, clambering stems. Flare of bold trumpet flowers.

Cushions of moss, massed and moist. Sandy touch of desert wind, gusts from mountain slopes. Salty whispers of rock island, jungle hoots.

Listen! Smell! Touch!
World in a tent.
Soon drunk on it, drowsed, bemused, bewitched.

Gilbert the vegetable grower had been coming to the Chelsea Flower Show for more years than he could count. This year he thought his display was the best ever – surely his peppers were the reddest, his onions the shiniest and his lettuces the leafiest in the whole marquee.

But it was hard work, these days. His back ached when he stooped to dig, or knelt to thin out seedlings. A helper, that's what he needed.

So when he glimpsed a small man in the marquee, a flicker of browny-green, something of bark and moss and rain about him, Gilbert looked and looked again. Something stirred in his memory – a whisper, an echo of a story he'd heard as a boy.

A pair of eyes, brightest green, peered back at him from behind a palm tree on the stand opposite.

It was his grandfather who'd told him – and he knew from *his* grandfather. Way, way back, time out of mind. Lob-lie-by-the-fire! Yes, it was coming back to him, that old, old story. Lob was the helper, the grower, fetcher of firewood.

'What, is he here for me?' Gilbert wondered. 'Oh, wouldn't that make life a whole lot easier? I'll go careful, mind. Don't want to scare him off.'

So, instead of looking back into that curious face, those sharp little eyes, Gilbert busied himself with his stand. He picked up an onion and polished it; he arranged radishes in a dish. From the corner of his eye he saw Lob watching his every move.

'He won't resist,' he thought, 'not for long.'

Sure enough, Lob crept closer. Soon he settled himself on the table, between a bunch of celery and a dish of beetroot.

Gilbert smiled. Nice touch, that! Might appeal to the public – those who could see, any rate. Most wouldn't; Gilbert knew that much. But for those who could, a stand with Lob on it – not a carving, not an ornament, but a real live Lob – would be a bit special! Impress the judges, too, if they had eyes to see.

So Gilbert stood beside his stand, arms folded, grinning broadly. He'd had the feeling his display needed an extra touch. Now here it was.

Just in time for the Royal Visit, too! The Queen always came to Chelsea, for a guided tour before the show opened.

Everyone bustled about, making sure all was ready. Every stand was groomed to perfection – every leaf tweaked, every speck of grit in place. No spilled earth must soil the floor. No snail must be crunched under the royal shoe.

The Great Marquee was quite dazzling. Plants and flowers lined the walls, climbed to the roof, and filled every bit of space with their colour and scent. There were palms and cacti, orchids and eucalyptus, carnations and sweet peas, leeks and parsnips, vines and trumpet lilies.

The TV cameras were ready as a fleet of shining cars pulled up at the main gate. Presidents and vice-presidents greeted the royal party and led them into the marquee.

Gilbert caught his breath. The Queen – yes, really! There she was, in a deep pink coat and hat. Behind her came Prince Charles, and various dukes, duchesses and

attendants. A TV cameraman walked back-
wards, anxious to keep the Queen in view
but not fall over his cable. Each gardener
stood ready to be introduced, and to answer
questions.

Her Royal Highness wouldn't visit all the
stands, of course, so Gilbert was astounded
when the procession approached his, and
the Queen paused to look.

He stood respectfully to one side.

'Delightful,' murmured the Queen; and,
'so beautifully arranged.'

'Wonderful to see so many varieties,' said
Prince Charles.

Gilbert felt quite puffed up with pride. Such compliments! The Queen and her followers strolled on to admire the next stand. As they did so, Prince Charles stopped, his eyes widening in surprise. Then he blinked and moved on.

He'd seen Lob! Surely he had.

But when Gilbert looked round to see what Lob was doing, he saw with horror that the neat pyramid of onions was spoiled. There, next to it, sprawled Lob – half a chewed onion in his hand, feet up, shedding earth from his boots. Bits of onion skin were scattered across the stand.

Quickly Gilbert selected a new onion from the box under the table, polished it on his trousers and put it in place; he brushed away the bits. Maybe the Queen hadn't noticed.

Everyone but Gilbert was still gazing at the royal party. He seized his moment, and grabbed Lob by one ear.

'Now then, you! That's enough!' he

hissed. 'Scoffing my onions! Messing up my display! Being disrespectful to the Queen! You need shutting up safely, you do!'

Behind his stall was a big hamper, which he used as a seat in quiet moments. He opened it up, dumped Lob in, then closed the lid and sat down hard.

'I know who you are – don't go thinking I don't,' he snarled. 'You can stay there till I decide what to do with you.'

From inside the basket, a furious scuffling could be heard by those who could hear. Then silence.

Late May

In Lucy's dream, Lob was everywhere. He was in the park, in the tiny garden behind the flats, in the trees that bordered the road. He was young, light as a grasshopper, shiny as a beetle, show-offy as a butterfly. In the gusts and showers of late May he darted about, touching a bud here, a leaf there. The candles of the horse chestnuts flared into brightness at his touch.

Lucy looked at it all, smelled and touched and listened, and was dizzy with delight.

Lob was here, and it was the beginning of summer. What could be better?

In the morning, when she woke up, she didn't even know she'd dreamed. She couldn't remember any of it. Wide-awake Lucy was pretending she didn't care any more, and she was starting to believe it.

May–August

When Gilbert the vegetable grower opened his hamper to check that Lob was still inside, he soon regretted it: Lob captured was an angry, writhing, struggling thing. Gilbert slammed the lid very hard.

With teeth-marks on his wrist and scratches on his arms, he thought it safer to keep Lob shut in. He lashed a strong rope around the hamper, and tied it in a triple knot. Two or three times each day, he opened the lid a crack to throw food in – a cabbage, or a bunch of radishes. There was no shortage of fresh vegetables.

When the showground was quiet, at night when all the visitors had gone home, he spoke to Lob in a whisper.

'I know you. I've heard of your sort. Couldn't believe my eyes when I seen you sat there on the stand, large as life. Would've let you stay – nice touch, I thought, make my stand a bit special – only you had to go and spoil it, din't you?'

There was no answer from the hamper. For a moment Gilbert thought Lob had escaped, but when he bent close and looked through the wicker, he was startled by a bright green eye staring back at him. There was a cold, glittery expression in that eye. Gilbert backed off quickly.

'Listen here, though,' he went on. 'How'd you fancy coming home with me? I could do with a helper, long as you behaves yourself. I'll give you a nice packing shed to live in. Greenhouse, if you'd rather. Good working conditions. Onions and fresh veg to eat, all year round. Can't say fairer than that, can I? How about it? Have we got a deal?'

Inside the basket, Lob had gone into a deep huff. He slumped, eyes closed. He didn't even glance at the vegetables Gilbert threw in.

He waited.

A few days later, the Show was over. All the hard work went into reverse – gardens were taken to pieces, trees and plants stowed back in lorries, even the Great Marquee was taken down. All that was left was trodden grass and mud where thousands of people had walked.

Gilbert had sold most of his vegetables, but what remained was packed into the back of his van, and Lob with it.

Chuckling to himself, Gilbert drove through London, heading north-east. He pictured his wife's surprise when he showed her what he'd got – that's if she could see.

Back at home, he boasted, 'I spoke to the Queen! The Queen! And she stopped for a chat with me. Said my stand was the best in the whole show, best by miles. And look what I've got here! A new helper. See – only be careful. It bites.'

'What is it – a dog?' said his wife, peering into the hamper.

'Not a dog, a Lob. A Lob-lie-by-the-fire. You know! A helper.'

'Pfff!' went his wife, seeing nothing but a few wilted cabbage leaves. 'Aren't you a bit old to be playing silly games?'

Gilbert took no notice. He carried the hamper into his packing shed, where he intended to keep Lob shut up. At first, anyway; he didn't want him straying. Things would sort themselves out. Lob would come round to his way of thinking.

He had a big old run where he had once kept a guard dog, a grumpy Alsatian. It would do for now.

This cage was in the large shed where strawberries and salad crops were brought in crates and boxed up to be sold. Gilbert's workers did the picking and packing, but none of them saw Lob. At night, Lob was supposed to sort and pack the fruit Gilbert put into his cage.

'That's your way, isn't it?' Gilbert said. 'Get

on with your jobs when no one sees.'

Lob was NOT going to work for Gilbert.
Not a single strawberry would he touch,
not a stalk or a pip of one. Gilbert tried
coaxing, cajoling, even threatening, but
nothing worked.

'Go on, have your sulk!' Gilbert told
him, getting impatient. 'You'll have to come
out of it sooner or later.'

Lob didn't. All he did was fret and pine.

Imprisoned!

Locked in. Caged. Strong bars. Cold hard floor that reeks of dog.

Shut away from the air, from the grass and rain. Snarl and gnaw, scratch and claw. No battering will bend those bars. No terrier could tunnel through that floor.

Won't work.

Can't sleep.

Won't eat.

Can't rest.
Fade thin as a leaf.
Scarcely move. Only
half alive.

Days went by. Days and days and days.

Looking into the cage, Gilbert frowned.
This wasn't working. He offered Lob
asparagus, spinach, and succulent lettuce.
Not a leaf or a stalk of it would Lob touch.

Gilbert felt uneasy. Wherever he went,
glassy green eyes seemed to drill
into him.

One morning
Gilbert unlocked
the packing shed
and called
out, as usual,
'How are we
today, then?

Bright-eyed and bushy-tailed?'

Silence, as he expected. But what he didn't expect was to find Lob sprawled on the cage floor, lifeless as a pile of rags.

'Oi! Lob-lie-by-the-fire!' There was a touch of panic in Gilbert's voice. 'Lazybones! Stir yourself!' He nudged Lob with his foot; bent down and poked him. Not a flicker.

'Blessed if the varmint hasn't gone and died on me,' he muttered. He stood for a moment wondering what to do.

No one must know about this; that was for sure. Better bury the useless creature before anyone found it and accused him of starving it to death.

He fetched a shovel, and began digging behind the compost heap. It needn't be much of a hole, for such a pathetic, shrivelled corpse. Returning to the packing shed, he picked up the raggy thing, bundled it in his arms – how light it was, almost weightless! He couldn't look at it closely, for fear that those sharp eyes might open and stare back.

It made a dry rustling sound as he dumped it in the hole. He shovelled earth over and stamped it down hard.

Then he tried to forget all about it.

Gilbert didn't sleep well that night. In his dreams, glittery green eyes jabbed and poked at him.

August

When Lucy heard Mum and Dad talking in their bedroom, she couldn't help listening. She stood by the door, ears alert. It was eavesdropping, she knew it was, but she couldn't help it.

It was something Dad said that made her stop to hear more.

'Have you heard anything about Lob, lately?'

What? They were talking about Lob?

No, they weren't. They were talking about *her*.

'No,' said Mum, after a pause. 'Not since she went back to school. She hasn't mentioned him for a week or two, at least.'

'Nor to me,' said Dad.

Was that relief in his voice, or a small sadness?

Now Mum: 'It's nothing to worry about if

she does! Lots of children have imaginary friends. Sometimes it goes on for years. It's Lucy's way of remembering Grandpa, all the fun they had together. If it helps her, that's got to be good.'

'Mm,' went Dad. 'I s'pose you're right.'

Then they went on to talk about boring things like whether to get a plumber in, for the leaky tap.

Silently, so that they wouldn't know she'd heard, Lucy tiptoed downstairs. *Imaginary friend?*

Lob? Is that what Lob was? What he'd been?

If he was imaginary, she thought, then Grandpa must have had a good imagination. Better than most people's.

Of course. Obvious. She'd gone along with Grandpa's game of make-believe; she'd pretended, because it made him happy.

She didn't believe in Lob. Never had done. Not really.

August

It had been hot all day, too hot. It was the kind of heat that rumbles itself up into a storm.

In the night it rained hard. At first, hot heavy drops spattered down on the dust. Thunder rumbled, far off. Then the rain fell and fell, with a steady hissing sound. The earth sucked it down greedily.

Under the ground, Lob was sleeping the kind of sleep he usually only slept in winter. He was no more dead than a bare oak twig is dead, or a bulb under the ground. Now, as warm rain seeped into him, he began to stir.

Bedded in earth, darkly blanketed. Wake to the wet warmth. Roots

tickle, rain trickles.
Hands unclench, push
up like a mole swims
in soil. Scoop away soil,
grapple with air. Legs
kick, clods fly, feet grip.
Head breaks surface . . .

Breathe, breathe!
Breathe the summer
night, the drenching
rain.

Stand, stretch, stamp.
Breathe. Live.

Lob waggled his head, clearing his ears of mud. He emptied out his boots, and put them on again, and wriggled his toes. His ears were alert for any sound from Gilbert's house, but there was none.

He was free. Ready to walk. The drenching rain made him strong again.

The grave was left as untidy as an unmade bed.

Past the dark house he went to the lane outside, and he stood there in the early dawn, sniffing, sensing his direction.

South. Something was pulling him south. That was the way the road led him.

He walked quickly until he'd put a safe distance between himself and Gilbert's packing shed. Then he slowed to his usual steady pace, neither hurrying nor dawdling.

Daylight came early; the rain cleared, and sunlight flashed on water. He reached a canal, with easy walking beside it, on a towpath. There were buttercups, and seeding grasses, and now and then the scurry and plop of a water vole.

Ahead, he saw the sprawl of buildings, the tall towers, the glittering windows. What he'd do when he reached the city he had no thought, but every step brought him closer.

Narrowboats chugged past, stopping at the wooden gates. Here the boat-people had to get out, open and close the gates with a great swooshing of water, and let their boats through.

Lob liked the look of those brightly-painted boats. The day had turned baking hot, and after a few hours of walking he thought he might ride on a narrowboat instead. He was hungry, too, after his days of refusing to eat. All he'd had today was watercress, and some bits of bread thrown for ducks.

He waited for the right boat.

The first to come by was too crowded, with music blaring. The second had three bothersome yappy dogs. The third had its

windows blinded, so he couldn't see inside.

All he wanted was a nice middle-sized boat, fresh-painted, with a bit of roof garden, and not too many people.

Before long he saw it.

One leap, and he was on board. Down some wooden steps he went, into a tiny kitchen. A saucepan of potatoes sat on a stove, waiting to be cooked. He took two, putting one in each pocket. A doorway led to a sleeping area, with bunk beds.

Lob was tired now. He yawned. Those beds looked tempting.

He went through, sat on the lower bunk champing his potatoes, then settled himself. Within moments he was fast asleep.

No one had seen the bedraggled, muddy, greenish-brownish man leaping aboard the Gipsy Rose.

Manda would have done, but she was asleep, sunbathing on the roof of the narrowboat.

Manda liked things neat. She liked things clean. She didn't like mess and muddle and dirt. She'd spent the morning cleaning and scrubbing and polishing the boat, inside and out. Now she was relaxing, while her husband steered.

She woke suddenly from a pleasant doze

with the idea that something was wrong. Standing up, she pushed her feet into flip-flops, and wrapped her towel round her.

There was a smell, a horrid smell. A whiff of something dirty and earthy and leafy.

Could a dog have got on board, a smelly dog? Or even a squirrel? She'd seen one of those, a nasty ratty thing, scuttling up a canal-side tree.

She looked along the boat's roof, past the pots of marigolds and herbs – no, nothing to be seen, only Matt's head at the stern end. He was whistling to himself as he steered.

Manda went down into the cabin, all her senses listening keenly. She heard snoring. Her eyes boggled. Yes, *snoring!* There it was – the Thing – lying peacefully asleep on Matt's bunk! A scruffy little tramp.

'Eurgghhh!' went Manda. 'Out! Get out!'

The Thing woke with a jolt, flung itself off the bunk and scrittered underneath like a cockroach.

Manda leapt up the steps and leaned on the roof, yelling: 'Matt! Come here! We've got a stowaway!'

Someone had to steer, so she took over while Matt went down to the cabin. When he came back, he was shaking his head.

'No! No one there. Are you sure?'

'Course I'm sure. It was a – a disgusting little man. Snoring on your bed, cool as you like.'

'Well, he's not there now,' Matt said, giving her a strange look.

Manda couldn't believe it. She made Matt moor up, and they both went to see.

'Is this a joke?' Matt lifted a cushion and peered underneath.

'No. He's in here, the verminous creature. I can *smell* him – can't you?'

Matt made a show of checking everywhere – in the cupboard, on the overhead rack, under the bunk. 'Nope,' he said. 'Definitely no one here. I'm going back up. Let me know if we're boarded by pirates.'

'Hmmff!' went Manda.

She waited till Matt had restarted the engine. Then she fetched a torch, got down on all fours and peered under the bunk. Yes! Eyes green as bottle-glass stared back at her.

'*I* can see you,' she hissed, 'even if *he* can't. Come on out!'

She didn't want to touch the horrid Thing, but there was nothing for it. She fetched rubber gloves, then knelt again, reached in and hauled it out.

It was far, far stronger than she'd expected. It wriggled and it struggled. She gripped more tightly, turning her face away and trying not to breathe. Up the steps she dragged it, and out to the deck. With a wince of disgust, she wrapped both arms tightly round the Thing, and picked it up.

'Over you go, revolting little object! *Ouch!*'

Just before she let go, it twisted in her grip and sank sharp teeth into her arm.

DUMPFF! PLUTT! Lob went, over the side. *HISHH – SPRRRR – GRAAAH!*

Tossed and churned, caught in the coils of oily water. Shapes lurk in murk. Whirled and swirled, limp as a strand of weed. Hands clutch, legs flail. Kick up, up. Bob like a cork, head surges into air. Gulp sweet mouthfuls.

Hands grip rusty

rungs. Clamber out. Spraddled, bedraggled. Crouch, retch, splutter and spit. Breathe. Breathe.

Sodden and gasping, Lob propped himself against a wall. For the second time that day he took off his boots and emptied them out.

All around him were buildings, railway lines and warehouses. The canal was a vein of water running into the city's heart. He'd arrived somewhere, at least; and it looked like city. There were people about, on boats, or walking their dogs, or just strolling or sitting. But no one looked his way.

Having been manhandled, kidnapped, imprisoned, buried, dunked and almost drowned, Lob was becoming very suspicious of people.

But wasn't he looking for someone?
Wasn't that why he'd come?

He shook canal water out of his ears, and
tried to remember.

August

It was the summer holidays, the time when Lucy usually went to stay with Granny and Grandpa. This year would be different, but still Lucy was going to Clunton, to visit Granny Annie at Forge Cottage, where she lived now.

'Do I have to go?' Lucy grumped, the night before. 'I'd rather stay at home.'

'Lucy!' Mum was packing Lucy's bag. 'You know how Granny Annie loves having you. You can't disappoint her.'

'But it won't be the same.'

'No, Lucy-Lu, it won't.' Mum gave her a hug. 'It's not the same for Granny, either.

But you can help her remember Grandpa. She'll like that.'

For the whole of the long car journey, Lucy brooded in the back seat. It wasn't the same. Clunny Cottage wasn't even there any more. Grandpa Will was gone. Everything was spoiled, nothing as she wanted it. It wasn't right.

At first, when they were clear of London, and the motorway cut through hills and fields, Lucy couldn't help scanning the verges, just in case Lob might be plodding along, heading south. But it began to seem silly, and she gave up.

Then there was the sadness of driving past the place where Clunny Cottage had been. It was demolished now, quite gone. The vegetable garden where Grandpa Will and Lob used to work had disappeared altogether; in its place were brand-new houses, two-thirds built.

Forge Cottage was very different – smaller

and prettier than Clunny, in a row of others, and in the main village street. When she'd forgiven it for not being the cottage she was used to, Lucy began to like it. Granny Annie had neighbours, and she could walk to the Post Office and shop, and it was much better than being two miles away, all on her own. The garden was only a small one, and Granny Annie paid the postman's son to come and tidy it once a fortnight.

There wouldn't be enough for Lob to do, Lucy thought. There was no scuff or rustle of Lob in this little garden. It wasn't a Grandpa place, either. Because Grandpa Will had never lived here, it didn't feel quite as if he'd gone. Just that he was busy somewhere else, and might turn up soon.

At school Lucy's class had been making collages, and she decided to make one as

a present
for Granny Annie. She collect-
ed scraps of fabric, she cut out shapes from
magazines, she collected seeds
and beans and bits of green ribbon
and wrapping paper.

She hadn't
quite decided
what sort of
pattern to
make, but as
she pushed
things around on
her paper and
reached for the
glue, she found
that they were
making themselves
into a face.
A Green Man face,
full of mischief
and knowingness.

'It's not really Lob,' she told her grand-mother, 'but it's a bit like him.'

Granny Annie was delighted. 'Well, just look at that! Wouldn't your Grandpa have loved to see it! Is it really for me? I'm going to get it framed, and have it up on the wall.'

She wasted no time in getting the Green Man mounted and framed, and soon he was grinning above the fireplace. Everyone who came to the cottage was shown him, and invited to admire Lucy's work.

'What a little artist my Lucy is! Isn't she a clever girl?'

Lucy was glad that her grandmother was so pleased, but a bit sorry to leave the Green Man behind. She decided that when she got home, she'd make another, for herself.

When Mum and Dad came to collect her, and she turned at the door for one last look at the Man, she almost thought he winked.

Late August

Through the city streets Lob walked.

He was in a mad, noisy place, full of rush and hurry. Cars and lorries and buses growled past, and the pavements were thick with people-traffic. He was hemmed in on all sides, by buildings and roads. Not a tree could he smell, and the sky was chopped into angular shapes.

He followed the current of people to an island in the traffic, a huge stepping stone. Lights flashed red, then yellow. Then the light became a small green man, walking.

Lob had stepped out into the road, but now he stood and stared until the green man faded, replaced by a standing red one. Now vans and lorries were surging at him, snarling. A van brushed against him, swirling him aside like a leaf. Lob leaped for the other side and stood there panting, as if he'd hauled himself out of a churned and treacherous river.

The people hurrying along the pavements didn't look up at the sky, or notice the pigeons and starlings that fluttered above their heads. They didn't glance at Lob, or at each other; they were too busy striding, heads down.

Men in yellow had fenced off part of the

road ahead. The traffic formed a growling pack. Lob's instincts warned of danger.

He wasn't frightened of much, but this was something new and terrifying. Still, curiosity drew him closer. Part of the road had been gouged up, its intestines bared. One of the yellow men jumped into the hole. He picked up a heavy metal tool that racketed into life, throbbing, probing deep.

The noise juddered through Lob's bones.

Stop . . . STOP!
Head-crashing
Ear-cracking
Mind-bursting
Thought-snapping
Heart-booming
Feet-clamping

Bone-jarring
Sense-crazing
MADNESS . . .

Even the people on the pavement found the noise unbearable. They winced at the din, and clamped their hands to their ears. They hurried on by, trying not to breathe.

No one noticed a small, scruffy man, a bit green, a bit brown, a bit tattered, and very startled, clamped in fear by the side of the road. No one saw him bolt into the entrance of the Underground station.

But as Lob teetered at the top of the escalator, someone did see. A very small person called Frankie.

Frankie liked those moving staircases. He liked the way they glided out from under his feet, then dropped into steps. He liked watching the picture-show on the walls on the way down. He even liked scaring himself by thinking what might happen if he didn't get off in time, and was sucked through the teeth at the bottom and under and round and up to the top again, slithering out as a Frankie-pancake.

'Hold my hand,' said Mummy, and he held tight. She'd folded up the buggy, and had it in her other hand.

He'd been frightened, the first time Mummy let him stand instead of being carried, to find himself swept down between smooth walls, without moving his feet. So when he saw the green-brown muddy man hesitating at the top, he understood at once that here was someone who hadn't seen sliding stairs before.

As he and his mother approached, the man turned, saw them, and stepped aside.

'Aggit!' Frankie said, with a friendly wave.

'Yes, darling,' said his mother. 'Escalator, that's right. No need to be scared.'

Frankie turned to watch as they rode down. The man followed. But he didn't look at all sure, and was scrabbling with his hands, trying to get a grip on the side wall.

'Come on, Frankie. Don't drag behind,' Mummy said, at the bottom. She lifted the buggy clear, and they turned left to their platform.

Which way would the mud-brown green man go? Frankie loitered, and saw him pitch forward, not knowing he had to step off. He lay spreadeagled like a frog. Frankie yelled out, and tried to drag his mother back.

'No, Frankie! This way.'

The muddy man picked himself up, looking cross, then followed. Frankie's mother always kept him well back from the platform edge, but the man didn't notice the drop until he was teetering above the dark ditch where the rails ran.

'Own! Own't!' shouted Frankie, but his words didn't always come out the way he meant. Mum thought he was pointing at the big poster on the tunnel wall.

'Passengers are reminded to keep all belongings with them,' said a loud voice. 'Please mind the gap when boarding.'

Now the man had leaped back, and the train came swooshing in, with a blast of hot tunnel air. One of Frankie's scaring-himself games was to pretend that the train was a monster roaring out of the darkness, that opened all its mouths to swallow him. His legs went quivery. What if it *was*?

'Oh, it's not too full,' said Mummy. 'Plenty of seats.'

It was safe after all. They got on. Mummy opened up the buggy, sat Frankie in it and fastened the straps.

'Ook! Ook!' He looked round wildly for the mud-green man, and saw him huddled under a bench on the platform.

'Yes, I know. It won't be long,' said
Mummy. 'Only eight stops.'

Frankie saw green, green eyes staring back
at him; he smiled and waved. If he'd known
enough words, he'd have said, 'Come with
us! It's OK. I've done it loads of times. You
don't have to be scared.' What came out was,
'Ugglebuss!'

At the last moment, just as the doors
began to gasp themselves closed, the man

squirmed out from under the bench, and
bolted into the carriage.

'Eep! Eep!' Frankie squealed in delight.

'It's only the doors closing, Frankie,' said
Mummy.

The brown-green man looked up and
down the length of the carriage, then
crouched on the floor near Frankie. Frankie
squeaked and laughed, and waggled his
fingers. No one else took any notice. The
other passengers were reading their
newspapers, dozing, chatting, looking at
their fingernails.

'Look! Here's Muffet,' said Mummy,

twirling the fluffy blue cat out of her bag.
'Play with Muffet.'

Frankie didn't want Muffet. He had a new
friend now. The train moved off into black-
ness. The brown mud man tried to dig into
the floor with his nails. Soon the train had
rushed into the brightness of the next
station; people got off, people got on.
The man, buffeted by feet and legs, clung
tight to the buggy. Then he clambered
into an empty seat opposite. Frankie waved
and kicked.

The train whizzed into the whooshy
dark, and now the man was boggling
at his reflection in the black
window.

'Week!' Frankie tried to
explain, but the greenyman
wasn't listening.

Another stop,
and the carriage
filled up. A nice

lady smiled at Frankie, and someone else tried to sit on top of the man.

'An!' Frankie warned.

Spluttering in outrage, the man wriggled free. Frankie could hardly see him now, there were so many bags and briefcases and standing people.

The man was going. Ducking between legs, under elbows and over bags, he was past Frankie and out on to the platform as the doors squeezed shut.

'Eye bye,' said Frankie, sadly. And as the train moved on, he began to cry loudly for the loss of his friend.

No matter how flustered his mummy was, no matter how she tried to console him with Muffet and tickling, he wept and he sobbed and he bawled.

Lob stood panting on the platform. It wasn't safe down here.

The roarer sighed, clamped its mouths,

and slid away. Lob stood on the platform in the echoing quiet.

He wasn't easily scared, but he hadn't liked being in that tunnel-snake. The thought of being trapped underground, away from air and trees and wind, was the worst of all possible fears, for Lob. Being dumped in oily water and buried in shallow earth had been quite pleasant, compared to that.

How to get out, back to the air?

Round a corner he saw more of those gliding steps. He climbed on. Ahead, daylight showed him the way to freedom. He crawled under the slapping-gate, climbed some steps, and found himself out under the sky, breathing real air. *Air*. City air, but better than the black dusty stuff trapped underground, and the hot snake breath.

This was another busy street, but now the cars and the buses and the people hardly bothered him at all. Not after the adventure he'd just had. He felt brave, heroic. He stepped out, with a bit of a swagger. These people had no idea what dangers he'd faced, or how clever he'd been to escape.

Walk. That was the thing. Nothing like it.

Beyond the canyon of buildings, he sensed grass, and trees, and water. It cheered him. People built their cities, they covered acres of land with concrete, they dug roads and snake-tunnels. But always there'd be green and wildness beyond.

When he reached a pair of big gates standing open, and a path leading across grass, he turned in and walked towards a lake. Beside the path was a splendid beech tree, grown proudly to full height. Cool shade spread beneath its branches, an invitation.

Lob couldn't resist. Leaning comfortably against the trunk, he slept.

Late August

At home, Lucy had made another Green Man, this time for herself.

She made it in reds and golds and bronzes – autumn colours – and studded it with berries.

Then she made a winter one, frosted and pale, with bristling eyebrows. Soon she had four, one for each season.

Mum and Dad thought they were marvellous, and mounted them on the wall. Mum's friend Sue saw them when she came to tea, and liked them so much that she asked Lucy to make one for her, too. Then Lucy thought of making birthday cards for all her friends.

Each one was different: the colours, the patterns, the fabrics she chose, and the buttons and berries and seeds she used for decoration. The faces were different, too.

But each one, when she caught sight of it in the corner of her eye, seemed to look back at her. I'm here, it seemed to say. Always here.

'How imaginative!' people said. 'How clever you are, Lucy! Are you going to be an artist when you grow up?'

Lucy stopped to think. She liked the idea that all the possible choices in the world were spread in front of her like sweets on a counter, and she could have whatever she wanted. Dog-handler? Film star? Astronaut? She might be this. She might be that. There was no need to decide, not for a long, long while.

Late August

If you'd been in the park that day, you might have passed a group of teenagers, two boys and two girls.

They were Alison and her friends, with the afternoon to themselves. They walked slowly, because they liked being together and had no reason to hurry.

They walked quite close to the beech tree, but only Alison noticed. What she saw – thought she saw – was a greeny-brown heap, huddled against the trunk. At first she thought it was a pile of rags someone had left, but a second look showed her a gnarled, sleeping face.

In her memory, something stirred – something she couldn't quite get hold of. A story, a dream, someone she'd met ages ago?

She broke off what she'd been saying to Priya, and approached the tree.

Eyes opened and looked at her:
bright eyes in a craggy face.

'Oh!' she exclaimed. 'Sorry – I
didn't mean to wake you. It's you,
isn't it?' The words were out before
Alison knew what she meant. 'Where've
you come from? Where are you going?
Are you tired? Are you hungry?'

A deep happiness glowed through her.
The greenish man gave no reply, but she
knew he was listening intently.

'You're here for me,
aren't you?' she whis-
pered. She crouched
on the grass.
'Waiting. That's
why *I'm* here—'

Her friends
waited, bored.
Jason kicked
at a fallen
twig; Craig

had taken out his mobile.

'Come on, Ali,' called Priya. 'What you looking at?'

Alison twisted round. 'At *him*! Come and say hello!'

She saw Priya glance at Jason, puzzled.

'You know what she's like.' Jason made a *durr* face. 'She'll be yattering away to a beetle or an earwig.'

But they drifted over. Alison saw wariness on the small man's face. He was fading to the colour of beech bark.

'See? See him? What now, though? What shall we do? We can't leave him here.'

'Ali,' said Craig, 'what you on about?'

'Winding us up. As usual.' Jason flopped down on the grass, flinging his arms back and almost whacking the small man on the ear.

'Careful!' Alison pushed him aside.

'What?' Jason grumped.

'If you just tell us,' said Priya. 'What is it?

A pigeon or something?'

'What's the matter with you lot?' Alison huffed. 'Can't you see? Right here by the tree?'

Priya stood hand on hip, head tilted. 'Yeah, what are we gawping at?'

'Have you had your eyes tested lately? He's right there! A – a man, look.' She pointed. 'Sort of greenish, old – come on, I'm not making this up! You're just pretending, aren't you?' She looked at each of their faces in turn; saw amusement flicker from one to another, as if they were ganging up on her.

'Little green man, yeah, yeah,' muttered Jason. 'From the planet Zarg, right? His flying saucer's parked over there. Better watch out – he might take us hostage.'

'No! Not that sort of green man.'

'Little green pixie sitting on a toadstool?' said Craig.

'No! Not that sort of green man, either,'

Alison insisted. 'Come on! You're not looking properly.'

Priya giggled. 'All we can see is you gawking into thin air.'

Jason made a *screwy* sign, one finger against the side of his head. Then he jumped for the tree's lowest twigs, grabbed a handful of leaves and ripped them off, scattering fragments on the grass. He reached for a branch and hung on with all his weight, swinging, scuffing his feet.

Alison winced. 'Don't!'

'Come on, Ali,' said Craig. 'You've had your joke. Very funny, ha ha. Let's go. I want an ice cream.' He tugged at her arm.

'Ow. Get off!' she protested, pretending

not to like it. She twisted away, and narrowed her eyes at the greenish man. She saw only a mossy, barky blur now, smelled only a hint of earth and leaves. Then she blinked him away altogether.

She laughed, and let Craig pull her up.

'Course there's nothing there!' she told her friends. 'I mean, little green men? Had you fooled for a minute, though, didn't I?'

And, looking back one more time, she saw nothing at all.

Lob watched them go across the grass, laughing, pushing and shoving each other, friends together.

The girl – so promising she'd seemed! Blue eyes full of friendliness. Her pretty face, shaded by a pink hat, glowed with interest and delight. She knew him at once. But then, when the others surrounded her . . .

He saw something he'd never seen before. Into her face came the determination not to see – not to want to see. She made herself see only what she expected to see. Her eyes seemed to glaze over; they looked through him.

In his long life, Lob had met many people, more than he could count. Hundreds and hundreds who didn't see him, and the rarer ones who did. But never before had he known someone decide – actually decide – not to see him.

He made himself stand, and walk, with no sense of any direction being better than any other. His steps wavered.

Shrunk. Faded. Pale as a cobweb, frail as a husk. Last leaf that clings to a twig. Not-seeing eyes that blank and shrivel. Eyes that lie, deny.

Go. Walk. One step and another.

Walk. Walk. Find . . . must find . . .

Thoughts blur.

Only later, in bed at home, did Alison feel a twinge of loss.

She kept thinking – half-dreaming – of the park, the tree, the green eyes that seemed to speak to her. It was like meeting someone she'd known for years and years, someone she could know for ever. If only the others hadn't been there . . .

Next day, on her own, Alison went back to the park and hurried across the grass.

Which tree
had it been?
This one?
That one?
But no shabby
figure waited under
any of them. Maybe
she'd only dreamed
him.

September

'I wish we had a garden,' said Lucy. 'Couldn't we move to a house with a garden? I want to grow things.'

'Oh, Lucy! Dad and I would love a garden of our own,' Mum said, 'but we just can't afford it, in London. And we have to be in London for our jobs.'

Mum and Dad were trying to get an allotment, but there was a waiting list.

'You can still do a bit of gardening, Lucy-Lu,' said Dad. He had a stone sink and some pots outside in the tiny courtyard, where he grew herbs – he was Grandpa Will's son, after all. 'We'll get you some pots of your own, and some seeds. I'll help you.'

They went to the garden centre, and chose a window box and a large pot for Lucy. They bought seeds, and bulbs – crocuses and daffodils and dwarf irises – to come up in the spring.

'Next year you can sow seeds in pots indoors, on the window sill,' Dad told Lucy, 'to go outside when the weather's warm enough.'

They spent a long time looking at the packets of seeds – rows and rows of them, with pictures of bright flowers. Lucy thought of sowing beans with Grandpa, how carefully he tipped them and tucked them in. She shook her seed packets, and heard the dry rattle inside. She smiled, and remembered.

Lucy had her birthday at the end of the summer holidays. Granny Annie, hearing of her new interest,

bought her a little trowel
and fork, and a watering
can.

September came, and
school started. Now,
every afternoon when she
came home, Lucy went
out to the yard to water her
pots, and to see if anything
new was sprouting. On warm nights she
opened her bedroom window, and leaned
out to smell the growing.

She didn't talk of Lob
any more, but on
her bedroom
wall a Green Man
seemed pleased
with the new
developments.

September

It was the start of a busy Monday. People set off in their cars to sit in traffic jams. They waited for buses. They pushed buggies along the pavements and delivered children to school.

For Lob, the day was hours old. He was walking. He'd forgotten where he was going and why. Now he just followed his nose, and his nose had brought him to a part of the city made mainly of houses.

Excited voices drew him to a school playground where children ran and skipped and hopscotched. This cheered him, and he paused to watch until a loud bell rang, and the children filtered inside. The voices faded, and Lob walked on.

Today was grey and cool. Feeling the first drops of rain, he tilted his face to the sky.

Harder and harder it rained. Drops plinked from leaf to leaf. Water pit-patted, gutters gurgled. Flowers and shrubs reached out and drank and were thankful.

But the people – how stupid they were when it rained! They seemed horrified. Instead of standing out in it to be watered and refreshed, they squealed and ran for cover. Some held up umbrella-sticks or pulled hoods over their heads. Lob sneered. How did they survive, knowing so little? Did they think they could live without rain?

He plashed on through puddles, boots

squelching. For a mile or more he walked, and then . . .

A narrow path, well-trampled. Fence, bindweed clinging. Space beyond, smells that beckon. Bonfire ash, compost, manure. Wet grass, wet soil, wet leaves.

Breathe.
Breathe it all in.
  Beanpole tents.
  Stripes of lettuce.
Ferny carrot-tops,
strawed strawberries,
tendrilly peas. Tool
sheds and barrows,
heaps of clippings.
  Leafgreen grassgreen
mossgreen wetgreen
greengreen.
  A place that welcomes.
A place to stay.

Cornelius was singing to himself, in his creaky old man's voice, as he walked steadily towards his allotment.

Twelve paces to the corner; turn left. Twenty paces to his shed. Touch the corner with his stick. Round to the front.

He knew at once that someone was there. Cornelius' eyes saw nothing, but still he knew.

Someone was there. Someone ageless. Someone he remembered, deep inside himself.

'Who there?' he called, balancing himself on his stick.

He listened closely, facing the pile

of sacks under the lean-to part of his shed. His ears, almost as good as eyes, heard the someone sitting up and yawning.

'Who there?' he asked again.

Lob. My name's Lob, came the answer. The whispering, reedy voice sounded as if the Someone wasn't used to speaking aloud.

'Lob, you say? You very welcome. My name Cornelius – very please to make your acquaintance, Mr Lob.'

You can hear me?

'I hear you faint,' said Cornelius, 'but you there.'

No one's ever heard me before. No person. Some folk see, but they don't hear.

'Then,' said Cornelius, 'I guess it make sense that I hear but don't see. Seems fair to me.'

Most folk don't see nor hear.

'That make sense, too,' Cornelius chuckled. 'Lot of folk don't see nor hear what's in front of they noses. You come a long way?'

*A long, long way. Days and nights and days.
I don't know how far.*

'And where you heading?'

I never know till the road takes me there.

Cornelius nodded. 'Good way to travel.'
With his stick and his free hand, he felt his
way towards a plank seat against the shed.
Carefully he sat. When he was settled, with
his stick placed by his feet, he patted the
bench beside him. 'Well, Mr Lob! Looks
like the road brought you here. You
welcome to rest you bones, and take the
air with me.'

Thank you, Mr Cornelius.

'Just Cornelius is fine. No Mister.'

Just Lob, then. No Mister.

Cornelius heard Lob settle beside him,
light as a leaf. A blackbird sang close by.

Good. A good patch of ground.

'This my patch,' Cornelius said proudly,
spreading his hands to the square plot in
front of him, bordered by a grass path. 'Not

big, but it keep me out o' mischief. I come
here every day, rain or shine. See, I got
tomatoes, and spinach, and callaloo. In the
frames over there I got peppers and squashes
and eggplant. I got beans and red peas. I
look after them, they look after me.'

But you can't see.

Cornelius nodded. 'My hands do the

seeing. Hands, nose. And I got my—'

'Granpa! Granpa!'

Two children came running, criss-crossing the paths.

'My grandbabies.' Cornelius' lips parted in a beaming smile. 'My Benji and my Zirvana – Zivvy, we call her. They come every day from school.'

He stood up, and swept both children into a big hug. They giggled and wriggled.

'Granpa, we made cake!' Zivvy was rummaging in her rucksack. 'Coconut and mango – yumptious! Mine fell to bits, but Benji's didn't.'

'That's 'cos you drop the tin.'

'I didn't! Sumira pushed me —'

'Listen, child. Listen, both.' Cornelius held up a hand. 'We got a visitor today – don't you see him?' He turned to the bench.

There was a silence. A searching silence.

'But, Granpa,' said the girl. 'Nobody here 'cept you and us.'

'Maybe he gone,' said the boy.

I'm here. I'm still here.

'No, I think he shy,' said Cornelius. 'Don't let's frighten him 'way. Maybe he show himself in a while.'

They all had jobs to do. The children put down their rucksacks by the shed. Benji emptied the wheelbarrow of clippings, Zivvy fetched a tray of tomato seedlings and a stack of pots. Cornelius scooped soil out of a sack, and sat on his bench to pot up the little plants. The children told their grandfather about their day, the lessons they'd had at school, the games. They talked very fast, often both at once. Cornelius smiled and nodded.

Soon, his ears told him that Lob was helping – firming the tomato plants into their

pots, spreading their leaves.

Cornelius felt a deep, deep contentment, as if he'd met up with an old friend, a friend he'd known for ever. And Lob had met . . .

A man who sings to himself as he walks. Prods a stick to feel his way. Filmy eyes that gaze at nothing. Face keen and listening. Dark, dark skin, hair silvered grey.

Cracked voice sings of distant islands, of

waves breaking, of birds bright-plumed.

A happy man. A man with growing in his fingers.

September–Winter–Spring

At last, at last! Lob felt properly himself. Was this his journey's end? Was this what he'd been looking for, this allotment, this patch, this Cornelius?

And the children! Bright and keen, with their glossy dark skin, black hair and white, white teeth. The girl's hair was roped into tight rows like a corn doily. They made Lob feel as old as midwinter and as young as spring.

Lob stayed.

When Cornelius knew that this was how it would be, he went with his grandchildren to a car boot sale and bought a huge patchwork cushion. He put it in the shed, where it took up most of the space. Lob made himself a deep hollow in this cushion and slept warmly there, under the shelf of flower pots and twine and packets of seed.

Every morning, in first dawn light, Lob was at work. He moved down the rows of beans, weeded round the tomato plants, watered the peppers. Cornelius grew plants Lob had never seen before: callaloo, eggplant and squashes. But he soon learned what they wanted: how much water, how much sun.

Lob kept the watering cans full, and the tools bright and clean. Each trowel, rake and hoe had its own hook to hang on, where Cornelius' clever hands knew where to look.

'You know,' said Cornelius, 'this is going to be the best harvest ever. I feel it.'

Lob felt it, too. And the plants felt it, and the butterflies, and the bees. The squashes plumped up, the tomatoes reddened, and some of them split their sides with growing. The peas and beans ripened in their pods. Most days, after school, the children came, with their

197

overflowing energy.

Cornelius was always there, every day: the cool grey days, the plashing wet days and the days of baking sun. Each evening, when he'd finished watering and was ready to go home, he said, 'Thank you, friend Lob. Thank you kindly.'

Evening quiet, everyone gone. Work well done, and a bench to sit on. Work still to do. Cans to fill, tools to clean, weeds to pull.

Beetles skitter, snails

glide. Scritch of hedgehog. Fox's stealth. Countless tiny creatures busy being.

Roots reach under-ground. Stems push higher. Fruits and buds swell.

Listen. The song of the earth.

December came, and Lob shrank deep into himself, as he did in winter's depths. In hard frosty spells he went brittle and dry as a leaf, so deeply asleep that he wouldn't have woken if you'd nudged him with your foot. On milder days he stirred a little, and stretched, and smelled spring coming. If one of the gardeners had a bonfire, Lob crept out to warm himself by the blaze, and would stay there as long as there was a glow in the embers.

Then! Spring, and Lob was full of vigour again, young, sappy, his eyes sparking. He had extra work now, because Jake, whose allotment was next to Cornelius', was getting old, and found it hard to cope. But Lob had energy enough for two. He had no wish to sit about idle.

Spring, spring! Nature's extravaganza was everywhere – the life-giving, bird-nesting, egg-hatching, seed-sprouting, bud-bursting, leaf-greening summer carnival, when every living creature shouted BE! BE! BE! at the top of its voice.

But what about Lucy?

Part Three

April

A whole year had gone by since Lob left Clunny Cottage: a whole year of growing and seeding, fading and shrivelling, springing into new life.

A year wasn't much in the long, long life of Lob – nor, for that matter, in the rather long life of Cornelius. But in the short life of Lucy, a year was a big stretch of time. She was taller. The shoes she'd worn to the wedding didn't fit her any more. Her hair had grown, and she wore it differently.

Through the winter months, Lucy had little thought for gardening. She hardly glanced out of the window at her pots and window box waiting outside.

Then, quite suddenly in March, there was a different feel to the air. A tingle of expectation. The sky was streaked silver-blue. A blackbird sang in the tree by the park gates, and new shoots speared the soil. The pigeons seemed busy, strutting and cooing; the squirrel had a confident curl to his tail.

Lucy's pots knew it was spring, too. The bulbs had waited all through the winter with just the tips of their shoots showing. Now they were bright with colour: purple crocuses, yellow dwarf daffodils.

'We'll sow your seeds, soon,' Dad told Lucy, and she thought of Grandpa and the beans: how dried and wizened in the palm of his hand, but how much life was in them. She felt a tug of longing, happy-sad.

Usually the post brought only boring stuff, but this time:

'Brilliant news!' Dad waved a letter. 'We've got an allotment at last!'

They all went to see it. Their allotment. Their patch of ground.

On the way, Mum and Dad discussed plans for potatoes, onions and leeks, for raspberries, gooseberries and blackcurrants. The seasons rolled ahead of them as they walked and talked.

Lucy felt odd, as if her feet were leading her. She had a strange feeling of knowing where she was going, though she'd never been there before.

Dad had been given a plan, like a map, and he led the way along a grass path. And here it was: the smell of memories, and of Grandpa, and of happy days digging and planting.

The richness of dug soil. Earth and dampness and grass and growing. Shoots and stalks and new leaves; the promise of tight-furled buds. The scritch of something pecking in the shadows under a rhubarb plant.

Garden magic. The spell of it, deep and strong. All around, flowing into her.

Lucy breathed it all in. She heard a blackbird singing. She was dizzied.

Oh, she had forgotten! How good it made her feel, how *here* and *now* and *alive* . . .

Dad had found their plot; he stood looking at it, but Mum was distracted by the one next to theirs.

'Just look at this! So well cared for, and what amazing plants! I don't know what most of them are. Someone works hard here.'

'And how about ours?' said Dad. 'I was told it had got out of hand, but it's not that bad.'

'Perhaps someone's been helping,' said Mum.

Going over to look, Lucy heard Grandpa Will's voice in her memory. *Oh, he'll be about, somewhere or other,* he said, in his creaky, comfortable way. *Sure as ninepence.*

This was a Lob place, if ever there was one.

She stood still. She trembled. But just as she was about to whisper Lob's name, Dad called out to her; he was chatting to someone by a shed.

'Lucy! Come and meet Cornelius!'

Cornelius had the plot alongside theirs, the one that was tended and planted and ready to burst its boundaries, so full it was of glossy leaves and twining stems. As Cornelius stood up from his bench, Lucy saw his kind brown face and his silvered hair; she saw how his eyes seemed filmed over, and didn't look directly at her, but somewhere over her shoulder. Then she noticed how he felt his way, reaching with a stick, and she realized.

And even before she heard his deep voice with a creak in it, the Jamaican accent that at once she wanted to copy, Lucy knew that Cornelius was going to be their good and special friend.

'Welcome,' he said. 'Welcome, Lucy.' And he shook her hand, as if she were a grown-up.

'What a marvellous allotment!' said Mum, gazing round, reaching out to touch a leaf. 'How do you manage it all?'

'Ah, well,' said Cornelius, with a secretive smile. 'I have quite a bit of help.' And he

glanced towards the gooseberry bushes, as if
listening out for something.

Lucy looked that way too. There was a
quivering in the leaves, a dry scratching, and
then, just for a second, she saw – thought she
saw – a scruffy figure, in clothes the colour of
bark. She heard a scuffling that rustled like
laughter. And, looking out at her between
stems, a pair of bright eyes, green as new
acorns. She gave a little gulp. Was it? Could
it be?

'Is it you?' she whispered; and her ears thought they heard a rippling laugh. 'Is it? Have you come? Have you been waiting?'

Cornelius swivelled to face her; and she knew they were recognizing each other. Each knew that the other knew Lob.

But neither she nor Cornelius said anything, because Dad was asking what the various plants were, and Cornelius began to feel his way along the rows, pointing out callaloo, and the beds ready for bonnet peppers and speckled beans. And Lucy followed, and listened, and knew that this was the best place to be, in the whole of London. She hugged her secret, her wonderful, delicious secret. Lob was here. Lob! She'd called him, and he'd come. He was here, and so was she. And everything felt right. She knew it in her heart and her soul and her fingers.

September

And now?

Lucy comes to the allotment every week-end, and some days after school. She has her own part of it, her own rows; her own trowel and fork hang in the shed. She gets mud on her boots and soil under her fingernails, and is happy.

Courgette flowers flarc. Pumpkins and squashes squat like plump gold cushions. Speckled pods dangle. Everywhere is the purple and blue and maroon of cabbages, and green the brightest colour of all – shades of green, and the green of shade; green so vivid that it dazzles.

Sometimes Trudie comes, and Lucy has new friends as well – Zivvy and Benji, who are the same age as her but go to a different school. Lob would be a secret shared between Lucy and Cornelius, if it weren't for Zivvy

214

and Benji being in on it, too. Partly, at least. They play Lob games with their Granpa. They pretend, because they think he likes pretending.

'Is Lob here today, Granpa?' they ask. 'Where he hiding?'

'Up there,' Lucy tells them. 'See – quick!' And she points at Lob, up on the shed roof, where he's looking down at them all, chittering. But all they see is a roof, so they think Lucy's having a game with them. But Cornelius is smiling.

'Oh!' huffs

Benji. 'I want to see Lob. Why can't I?'

'And me!' Zivvy's not going to be left out.

'P'raps you will,' Lucy tells them. 'If you keep looking.'

But now she can't see Lob herself. Where is he? In the spinach? Between the raspberry canes? Up in the tree? Settling for a rest on the compost bin?

He's everywhere.

'Isn't it funny that Cornelius tells Lob stories to the children!' says Mum, walking home one Sunday afternoon. 'I thought Lob was Grandpa Will's invention. I always thought he made up the stories for Lucy – and for himself.'

'No, he used to tell me, as well, long before Lucy was around.' Dad's carrying bags of potatoes and onions, and leafy callaloo given him by Cornelius. 'I think it's an old, old story.'

'But some people know Lob's real,' says Lucy. 'Special people.'

And because she knows better now, she says it in a jokey way, so as not to give away the secret that belongs to her and Grandpa and Cornelius and Lob. She remembers what Grandpa told her, back in Clunny Cottage; she hears his creaky, comfortable voice, saying it. And it's as if he's still around, somewhere.

Lob's made of rain and wind. Sun and hail. Light and dark. He's made of fire and earth and air. He's made of grit and stones and stardust. Time gone and time waiting. The same stuff as all of us.

And Lucy knows that Lob is for ever and ever and ever, as long as the Earth is green.

Even if you haven't seen Lob, you'll probably see a Green Man, if you look, or sometimes a Green Woman. They're masked or caped or hooded in leaves. You might see one carved in a church doorway, looking out at you from stems and leaves of stone. They're everywhere. You might find one on a pub sign, or catch a glimpse of a face in the trees. You'll quite often meet them in gardens, of course; they like gardens. Some are majestic, some are friendly; some are stern, others mischievous. But each one has something of Lob about it.

If you come across one, try looking at it sideways, out of the corner of your eye.

It might be watching you back. They often do.

And next time you're in a wood or a garden, or near a tree or a hedge, be alert for rustlings and scritchings and scufflings.

Is that Lob? Is he there?

Maybe he isn't.

Maybe he is.

The End

Acknowledgements

With thanks, as ever, to David, Bella, Hannah and Linda, for patience, enthusiasm, insight and guidance. To Alison, Ben and Adele, for helpful suggestions. To Ness Wood and Pam Smy, for making the finished book such a beautiful thing. To Trevor, for many kinds of support. To Bernard Johnson, for my wise and companionable Green Man. To Michael de Larrabeiti, for *The Provençal Tales*. To Edward Thomas, of course. And to the man who walks the roads, who must have dropped a seed as he passed by. Thank you.

This is Linda Newbery's fifth story for David Fickling Books. Her first and second, *The Shell House* and *Sisterland,* were both shortlisted for the Carnegie Medal, and *Set in Stone* was the winner of the Costa Children's Book Award in 2006.

The author of more than thirty books for children and young adults, Linda is a frequent speaker in schools and at festivals and conferences, and tutors courses for writers of all ages. She lives in rural Northamptonshire.

Praise for Linda Newbery:

'Newbery writes wonderfully' *Financial Times*

'Newbery is an author who never lets her readers down' *Independent*